Outer Dark

CORMAC MCCARTHY is the author of ten acclaimed novels, most recently *The Road*. Among his honours are the Pulitzer Prize for Fiction and the PEN/Saul Bellow Award for lifetime achievement in American literature.

ALSO BY CORMAC MCCARTHY

The Road

No Country for Old Men

Cities of the Plain

The Crossing

All the Pretty Horses

The Stonemason
(a play)

The Gardener's Son
(a screenplay)

Blood Meridian

Suttree

The Sunset Limited

Child of God

The Orchard Keeper

CORMAC McCARTHY

Outer Dark

PICADOR

First published 1968 by Random House, Inc., New York

First published in Great Britain 1970 by André Deutsch

First published in paperback 1994 by Picador

This edition first published 2011 by Picador
an imprint of Pan Macmillan, a division of Macmillan Publishers Limited
Pan Macmillan, 20 New Wharf Road, London N1 9RR
Basingstoke and Oxford
Associated companies throughout the world
www.macmillan.com

ISBN 978-1-4472-1246-1

A CIP catalogue record for this book is available from the British Library.

Typeset by SetSystems Ltd Saffron Walden Essex
Printed and bound in the UK by CPI Group (UK), Croydon, CR0 4YY

Outer Dark

THEY CRESTED OUT on the bluff in the late afternoon sun with their shadows long on the sawgrass and burnt sedge, moving single file and slowly high above the river and with something of its own implacability, pausing and grouping for a moment and going on again strung out in silhouette against the sun and then dropping under the crest of the hill into a fold of blue shadow with light touching them about the head in spurious sanctity until they had gone on for such a time as saw the sun down altogether and they moved in shadow altogether which suited them very well. When they reached the river it was full dark and they made camp and a small fire across which their shapes moved in a nameless black ballet. They cooked whatever it was they had with them in whatever crude vessels and turned in to sleep, sprawled on the packed mud full clothed with their mouths gaped to the stars. They were about with the first light, the bearded one rising and kicking out the other two and still with no word among them rekindling the fire and setting their battered pannikins about it, squatting on their haunches, eating again wordlessly with beltknives, until the bearded one rose and stood spraddle-legged before the fire and closed the other two in a foul white plume of smoke out of and through which they fought suddenly and unannounced and mute and as suddenly ceased, picking up their ragged duffel and moving west along the river once again.

SHE SHOOK HIM awake into the quiet darkness. Hush, she said. Quit hollerin.

He sat up. What? he said. What?

She shook him awake from dark to dark, delivered out of the clamorous rabble under a black sun and into a night more dolorous, sitting upright and cursing beneath his breath in the bed he shared with her and the nameless weight in her belly.

Awake from this dream:

There was a prophet standing in the square with arms upheld in exhortation to the beggared multitude gathered there. A delegation of human ruin who attended him with blind eyes upturned and puckered stumps and leprous sores. The sun hung on the cusp of eclipse and the prophet spoke to them. This hour the sun would darken and all these souls would be cured of their afflictions before it appeared again. And the dreamer himself was caught up among the supplicants and when they had been blessed and the sun begun to blacken he did push forward and hold up his hand and call out. Me, he cried. Can I be cured? The prophet looked down as if surprised to see him there amidst such pariahs. The sun paused. He said: Yes, I think perhaps you will be cured. Then the sun buckled and dark fell like a shout. The last wirethin rim was crept away. They waited. Nothing moved. They waited a long time and it grew chill. Above them hung the stars of another season. There began a restlessness and a muttering. The sun did not return. It grew cold and more black and silent and some began to cry out and some despaired but the sun did not return. Now the dreamer grew fearful. Voices were being raised against him. He was caught up in the crowd and the stink of their rags filled his nostrils. They grew seething and more mutinous and he tried to hide among them but they knew him even in that pit of hopeless dark and fell upon him with howls of outrage.

In the morning he heard the tinker's shoddy carillon long through the woods and he rose and stumbled to the door to see what new evil this might be. There had been no one to the cabin for some three months, he himself coming harried and manic into the glade to wave away whoever by chance or obscure purpose should visit so remote a place, he himself slogging through the new spring mud four miles to the store and back once a week for such few things as they needed. Cornmeal and coaloil. And candy for her. When the tinker came rattling his cart in drunken charivari through the clearing he was there with wild arms like one fending back a curse. The tinker looked up, a small gnomic creature wreathed in a morass of grizzled hair, watching him with bland gray eyes.

Sickness here, he called. Got sickness.

The tinker took a few last short steps, backing into the wagon's momentum like a balky mule, halted and lowered the shafts to the ground and passed one ragged blue coat sleeve across his brow. What kind? he said.

The man walked toward him, still waving one hand, his pegged brogans noiseless in the thatch of pineneedles and the only sound in the clearing the tinker's pails penduluming with a tin clatter to gradual rest.

Old fevery chill of some kind, the man said. Best not to come round.

The tinker cocked his head. You sure it ain't the pox.

No. Done had the doctor. Said not to allow nobody around.

What is it. One of the youngerns?

No. My sister. Ain't nobody here ceptin me and her.

Well I hope her well anyways. You all need anything? Got everthing for the house from thread to skillets. Got some awful good knives. Got Dupont's powder and most ready-loads. Got coffee and tea for when the preacher comes. Got—the tinker lowered his voice and looked about him cunningly—got the best corn whiskey ye ever put in your thoat. One jar left, he cautioned with upraised finger.

I ain't got no money, the man said.

Well, the tinker said, musing. Listen. I like to help a feller out when I can. You got ary thing about the place you been lookin to trade off? We might could work up a trade some way. Somethin new and pretty might just set your sister up to where she'd feel better. I got some right pretty bonnets . . .

Naw, the man said, toeing the dust. They ain't nothin I need. I thank ye all the same.

Nothin for the lady?

Naw. She's mendin tolerable thank ye.

The tinker looked past him at the ruined shack. He listened to the silence in which they stood. Looky here, he said.

What is it, the man said.

He motioned with crook'd forefinger. I'll just show ye, he said. Here.

What is it?

The tinker reached down among his traps, groping in a greasy duck sack. He brought forth a small pamphlet and handed it slyly to the man.

The man stared at it, thumbed it open, riffled the crudely printed butcherpaper.

Can ye cipher?

Naw. Not good.

Don't matter noway, the tinker said. It's got pitchers. Here. He reached the book from the man and taking a confiding stance at his side flipped the book open to a sorry drawing of a grotesquely coital couple.

What about that? said the tinker.

The man pushed the book at him. Naw, he said. I don't want nothin. You excuse me. I got to see to my sister.

Well, sure now, the tinker said. I just thought I'd let ye take a peek. Don't hurt nothin do it?

Naw. I got to get on. Maybe next time you come thew I'll need somethin . . . He was backing away, the tinker still standing with the little book in his hand and the cupidity in his face gone to a small anger.

All right. Didn't mean nothin by it. I hope you'ns well. And your sister.

Thank ye, said the man. He turned and half lifted one arm in tentative farewell, then thrust both hands into his overalls and strode toward the cabin.

I'll be clost by a few days yet, the tinker called out after him. The man went on. The tinker spat and stepped again between the prone tongues and hoisted the cart and turned it, creaking and jangling, and set off again into the woods the way he had come.

The man had stopped short of the door and stood with one foot propped on the sill watching him out of sight. For a while he could hear the rattle and clang of the cart as it labored over the pocked and rutted road, fading, then ceasing into the faint clash of the pines and the drone of insects, and then he went in.

Culla, she said.

Yes.

That pedlar have ary cocoa?

No.

I sure would admire to have me a cup of cocoa.

She sat huddled in a ragged quilt, her feet gripping the bottom rung of the chair, watching the barren fireplace in which the noon light lay among the ashes and in which her voice trembled and returned about her.

He's done left, the man said. He ain't got nothin.

She stirred slightly. You reckon we could have us a fire tonight?

It ain't cold.

It turned cold last night. You said your own self it was cold. I sure do admire a good fire of the evenin. You reckon if it was to turn off kindly cool we could have us a fire?

He was leaning against the doorframe and slicing thin coils of wood away with his pocketknife. Maybe, he said, not listening, never listening.

Three days after the tinker's visit she had a spasm in her belly. She said: I got a pain.

Is it it? he said, standing suddenly from the bed where he had sat staring out through the one small glass at the unbroken pine forest.

I don't know, she said. I reckon.

He swore softly to himself.

You goin to fetch her?

He looked at her and looked away again. No, he said.

She sat forward in the chair, watching across the room with eyes immense in her thin face. You said you'd fetch her when it come time.

I never, he said. I said Maybe.

Fetch her, she said. Now you fetch her.

I cain't. She'd tell.

Who is they to tell?

Anybody.

You could give her a dollar. Couldn't you give her a dollar not to tell and she'd not tell?

No. Asides she ain't nothin but a old geechee nigger witch noway.

She's been a midnight woman caught them babies lots of times. You said your own self she was a midnight woman used to catch them babies.

She said it. I never.

He could hear her crying. A low bubbling sound, her rocking back and forth. After a while she said: I got anothern. Ain't you goin to fetch her?

No.

It had begun to rain again. The sun went bleak and pallid toward the woods. He walked into the clearing and looked up at the colorless sky. He looked as if he might be going to say something. After a while he licked the beaded water from his lip and went in again.

Dark came and this time he did have a fire, going out from time to time with the worn axe and splitting kindling and later by lanternlight scouring the near woods for old stumps which he split out and dressed of their rotted hearts, bringing in the hard and weathered shells and stacking them on the floor beside the hearth.

She was propped in the bed now with the frayed and musty quilt still about her. Periodically she would seize the thin iron headrail behind her, coming tautly bowed and slowly up with her breath loud in the room and then subsiding back among the covers like a wounded bird.

He had stopped asking her about it. He just waited, sitting in the chair and nursing the fire.

I wisht they'd hush, she said.

What.

Them varmints.

He drew the poker from the fire where he had been absently stirring the coals. Somewhere between the wind's cry and the long rip of rain on the tarpaper roof he heard a dog howl. They ain't botherin you, he said.

He heard her fingers clatter at the iron and her body rattle the springs as it arched. In a few minutes she said: Well I wisht they'd hush.

She wouldn't eat. He set a pan of cornbread on a brick before the fire and warmed it and ate with it the last of the cold meat he had brought from the store. He took the axe from under the bed and set forth one more time for wood. It was still raining but the wind had died and he could hear the dull lowing of an alligator somewhere on the river. When he came in again he stood the axe in the corner and stacked the wood and squatted once again before the fire. He was there for some time before she said his name.

What, he said.

Could you put it under the bed again? I believe it does ease it some. And it's for luck.

And toward morning she called him again.

Yes, he said.

What is it? Here.

I don't hear nothin.

Here. Over here.

He went to her. She put his hand on the crude tick.

Your water's broke, he said.

The rain had stopped and a gray light lapped at the window glass. There was no sound but the small patter of waterdrops on the roof, no movement but the slow wash of mist over the glade beyond which the trees rose blackly.

It's done mornin, he said.

I've not slept nary wink.

He was holding watch at the window, his own face drawn and sleepless. I believe it wants to clear, he said.

I wonder if they's ary fire in under them ashes.

He returned to the hearth and poked among the dead coals and blew upon them. I doubt they be a dry stick of wood in the world this mornin, he said.

The sun rose and climbed to a small hot midpoint in the sky. In the yard the man's shadow pooled at his feet, a dark stain in which he stood. In which he moved. In his hand a chipped enamel waterbucket now, headed for the spring, entering the woods where a path went and following it through kneehigh ferns, by rotting footlogs across a pale green fen and into a pine wood, scrub hardwoods, the ground soft with compost and lichens, coming finally to a cairn of moss-grown rock beneath which water issued limpid and cold over its bed of suncolored sand. He bent with the pail, watched with bloodrimmed eyes a leopard frog scuttle.

Coming into the clearing again he heard her call out. He crossed the glade rapidly toward the cabin, the water licking over the bucket rim and wetting the leg of his overalls. All right, he said. All right.

But that still wasn't it.

It hurts bad now, she said.

Then let's get on with it.

But it wasn't until midafternoon that she began. He stood before the bed in which she lay bowsprung and panting and her eyes mad and his hands felt huge. Hush, he said.

Cain't ye fetch her?

No. Hush.

The spasms in which she writhed put him more in mind of death. But it wasn't death with which she labored far into the fading day.

Late in the afternoon he rose and left her and walked in the glade. Doves were crossing toward the river. He could hear them calling. When he went in again she had crawled or fallen from the bed and lay in the floor clutching the bedstead. He did think she had died, lying there looking up with eyes that held nothing at all. Then her body convulsed and she screamed. He struggled with her, lifting her to the bed again. The head had broken through in a pumping welter of blood. He knelt in the bed with one knee, holding her. With his own hand he brought it free, the scrawny body trailing the cord in anneloid writhing down the bloodslimed covers, a beet-colored creature that looked to him like a skinned squirrel. He pinched the mucus from its face with his fingers. It didn't move. He leaned down to her.

Rinthy.

She turned her head. Far look and slow flutter of her pale lashes. I'm done ain't I? she said. Ain't I done?

Yes.

They Lord, she said.

When he picked it up it squalled. He took up the cord like a hank of strange yarn and severed it with the handleless claspknife he carried and tied it off at both ends. A deep gloom had settled in the cabin. His arms were stained with gore to the elbows. He fetched down some towels of wash-softened sacking and wet one in the waterbucket. He wiped the child and wrapped it in a dry towel. It had not stopped wailing.

What is it, she said.

What?

It. What is it.

A chap.

Well, she said.

It's puny.

Don't sound puny.

I don't look for it to live.

It sounds peart enough.

You best sleep some.

I wisht I could, she said. I ain't never been no tireder.

He rose and went to the door, standing for a moment in the long quadrangular light of evening, his elbow against the jamb and his head resting on his forearm. He opened his hand and looked at it. Dried blood sifted in a fine dust from the lines of his palm. After a while he went in and poured water into the tin basin and began to wash his hands and his arms, slowly and with care. When he came past the bed wiping his face with the towel she was asleep.

The child slept too, his old man's face flushed and wrinkled, small fingers clenched. Reaching down and refolding the towel about it he took it up in his arms and looking once again at the woman crossed to the door and outside.

The sand of the road was scored and banded with shadow, dark beneath the pine and cedar trees or fiddle-backed with the slender shade of cane. Shadows which kept compass against all the road's turnings. He stopped from time to time, holding the child gingerly, listening.

When he reached the bridge he turned off the road and took a path along the river, the swollen waters coming in a bloodcolored spume from about the wooden stanchions and fanning in the pool below with a constant and vicious hissing. He followed it down, carrying the child before him delicately, hurrying at a half-jog and keeping one eye skyward as if to measure against his progress the sun's, the deepening shade. Half a mile downriver he came to a creek, a stream of amber swampwater that the river sucked from high grass banks into a brief immiscible stain of dark clarity. Here he left the river and took a new course into the wood.

The country was low and swampy, sawgrass and tule, tufted hummocks among the scrub trees. He veered from the creek to gain drier ground, half running now, breaking through a patch of alder upon a small pothole out of which a heron exploded slowly and rose before him with immense and labored wingbeat.

Before dark he came upon the creek again, smaller and clear, choked with duckwort and watercress, the flat verdant ground stretching away everywhere beneath the sparse cover of trees and a coppery haze quivering like some rare dust in this twilight. The child had come awake again and begun to squall. He entered a stand of cottonwoods where the ground held moss of a fiery nitric green and which he prodded with his foot for a moment and then laid the child upon. It howled redgummed at the pending night. He stood back from it and watched it dumbly. It kicked away the towel and lay naked with legs pedaling. He knelt forward in the damp earth and covered it again and then rose to his feet and lumbered away through the brush without looking back.

He did not return along the creek but took his bearings by what faint light still lay in the west and struck out across country. The air was dank and stormy. Night fell long and cool through the woods about him and a spectral quietude set in. As if something were about that crickets and nightbirds held in dread. He went on faster. With full dark he was confused in a swampy forest, floundering through sucking quagmires and half running. He did not come upon the river but upon the creek again. Or another creek. He followed it down, in full flight now, the trees beginning to close him in, malign and baleful shapes that reared like enormous androids provoked at the alien insubstantiality of this flesh colliding among them. Long and long after he should have reached the river he was careering through the woods with his hands outstretched before him against whatever the dark might hold. Until he began to stumble and a cold claw was raking upward through his chest. When he came upon the creek again he splashed into it thigh and crotch before he knew it was there. He stopped, his breath roaring, trying to listen. Very far away lightning quaked once, again, soundlessly. The current moved dimly about him. He spat. His saliva bloomed palely on the water and wheeled and slid inexplicably upstream, back the way he had come. He turned and watched it in disbelief. He plunged his arm into the water. It seemed motionless. He spat again, and again the spittle flared and trembled and listed perverse. He surged from the water and began to run in the return direction and at a demented pace through the brush and swamp growth, falling, rising, going on again.

When he crashed into the glade among the cottonwoods he fell headlong and lay there with his cheek to the earth. And as he lay there a far crack of lightning went bluely down the sky and bequeathed him in an embryonic bird's first fissured vision of the world and transpiring instant and outrageous from dark to dark a final view of the grotto and the shapeless white plasm struggling upon the rich and incunabular moss like a lank swamp hare. He would have taken it for some boneless cognate of his heart's dread had the child not cried.

It howled execration upon the dim camarine world of its nativity wail on wail while he lay there gibbering with palsied jawhasps, his hands putting back the night like some witless paraclete beleaguered with all limbo's clamor.

IT WAS EARLY MORNING when the tinker appeared upon the bridge, coming from the woods with a sprightly hop like a stage dwarf after the main company has departed. He peered both up and down the road. Satisfied, he left the bridge and took the path along the river, going bowbacked among the rushes with his curious magelike agility. The sun was well up and the bracken along the shore steamed in the rising warmth. The tinker hummed a little air to himself as he went.

When he came to the branch where it joined the river he cast about for a crossing, coming finally to a narrows a short distance upstream. When he came back into the river path on the far side the tracks he followed had ceased.

Whoa now, he said. Which way we a-goin here?

He recrossed the creek and picked up the man's trace in a furrow of crushed ferns that led into the woods. Ah, he said. We a-takin to the deep pineys.

He lost the tracks more than once going up the branch but he paid that no mind. He was watching for tracks coming from the other way and he could find none. After he had gone a mile or so he ran out of any kind of track at all. He circled and returned, finding nothing. Finally he crossed the branch and went down the far side and very soon he came upon the tracks again. He followed them into a small clearing and here they ceased. He looked about him. It appeared to be the same place in which the tracks coming up the near side had vanished. As if their maker had met in this forest some dark other self in chemistry with whom he had been fused traceless from the earth. Than he heard the child cry. He turned, small grin among his wire whiskers. He found it at the far end of the clearing in a cup of moss, naked and crying no louder than a kitten.

Well well, he said, kneeling, you a mouthy chap if ye are a poor'n. He poked a finger at it as one might a tomato or a melon. Little woodsy colt ain't ye? Looks like somebody meant for ye to stay in the woods.

He folded the towel about it and picked it up and holding it against the bib of his overalls with one arm began his way down the creek again.

When he reached the bridge and the road he had not been gone two hours. The child blinked mindlessly at the high sun. The tinker entered the woods on the other side of the road where he had hidden the cart and searched among his goods until he came up with some cheap gingham in which to wrap the child. It drooped into sleep against his thin chest, its face mauve and wrinkled as though beset already with some anguish or worry. He placed it between some sacks in the floor of the cart and regarded it.

Well, he said, you alive if ye ain't kickin. He stooped and took up the tongues of the cart and set off through the woods, into the road, the wending trackless corridor down which echoed the clatter of his wagon and the endless tympanic collision of his wares.

He did not stop when he reached the store. He turned left onto the state road, going north now, moving with the same tireless pace. The child had not cried and he had not looked at it. Late in the afternoon he stopped to eat and it did cry, a thin and labored squall as he bent above it, his mouth slow and ruminative, chewing, dry cornbread collecting in his beard and sifting down upon the child. Tell em about it, he said.

When the sun had gone he went on in darkness, the child quiet again as if motion were specific against anything that ailed it. The moon came up and grew small and the road before him went white as salt. He jangled on through an iceblue light in his amulet of sound.

Before midnight he entered a town. Past a mill where a wheel rumbled drunkenly under its race and water fell with a windy slash. Past stores and shops, dark clustered houses, heralded and attended by the outcry of dogs down the empty streets and on again into the patched farmland. Another mile and he came to a wagon drive and a house a short way from the road that sat likewise in darkness. He pulled up before the door and lowered the cart to the ground. Halloo there, he called.

He waited. After a while light appeared very faint and yellow among the weather-riven slats and a woman's voice said: Who's out there?

Me, said the tinker.

Come in, she said, swinging open the door and standing there in a rough shift with a tallow candle in one hand.

He stamped his boots ceremonially once each on the sill and entered. Howdy, he said.

Late hours for a old man ain't it? she said.

It's late hours for a young one. I need me a nurse woman.

I've never questioned that.

No . . . here, don't shut the door. It's for this here youngern.

What youngern.

One I got in the cart. Bring that candle here.

She followed him out suspiciously and peered past his shoulder down into the cart where the child lay sleeping.

Looky here, he said.

They Lord God.

Here, let me fetch him out.

You take this candle, she said. I'll fetch him out.

It came awake with a thin yowl. She gathered it up and they went into the house and stretched it out on the crude board table, hovering above it nervously. Lord, she said, it ain't but just borned.

I know it, he said.

Where all did it come from?

I found it in the woods, he said. It'd been thowed away and I found it.

This poor thing needs fed.

I know it, he said. Is they ary nurse about here?

She was biting the backs of her knuckles. Mrs Laird, she said. She's just got her a new chap.

You reckon she'll take it?

She ain't got nary choice. Here, he needs better wrapped. Mind him a minute while I get some things and we'll go.

Where does she live at?

Just up the road. You mind him a minute.

Setting forth in the faint moonlight, the tinker now at her elbow and her carrying the child wrapped completely from sight, they appeared furtive, clandestine, stepping softly and soft their voices over the sandy road in shadows so foreshortened they seemed sprung and frenzied with a violence in which their creators moved with dreamy disconcern.

IT DID NOT rain again. He looked for it to, dark and starless as it was, coming down a road he could not see and through a wood kept by nothing he could hear. When he entered the glade a small hot moon came dishing up from the overcast to see him home. There was no light in the cabin. He stood for a moment with the rack of his chestbones rising and falling.

She was sleeping. When he emerged from the cabin again he was carrying the axe. He crossed the glade to the spring path and entered the woods. In a grove of blackhaws he stopped and looked about him and then sank the axe into the earth. He passed his shirtcuff across his forehead and took up the axe again and began to hack at the ground with crazed industry.

She had tried once to reach for the lamp but she could not move. She called his name softly in the quiet but there was no answer. The door was open and after a while he was standing in it, he and the axe in an assassin's silhouette against the slack gloss of the moon. He crossed to the table and took up the lamp and lit it, shaping the room from darkness. He turned to see her watching him, pale and disheveled and with such doll's eyes of painted china.

Culla? she said.

You best hope it's me.

Where you been?

Out.

Where's it at?

There was a long silence. He had not set the lamp down. He was holding the stained chimney in one hand and she could hear him breathing in the quiet. The flame trembling unhoused between them held her eyes.

It died, he said.

When she woke in the morning he was not there either. There was a small fire on the hearth and she watched that. He came in after a while bearing wood but he did not speak. He got the dipper from the waterbucket and brought it to her, helping her up with one hand, her neck craned, drinking, on her lips a white paste that clove to the dipper rim.

I want some more, she said.

He brought it. When she had finished she lay back and watched the fire again.

How you feel this mornin? he said.

I don't know. I don't feel much of nothin.

You'll be ailin some for a spell I would reckon.

I feel fevery.

You hungry?

I ain't real hungry.

You want eggs? I believe they's a egg.

If we got ary, she said.

There was one egg. He spooned lard into a pan and fried it over the fire and brought it to her along with a chunk of cornbread. I got to go to the store today, he said.

I got to go somewheres myself but I ain't able.

She was eating very slowly, her eyes on the plate.

Yes, he said. All right. I'll get somethin.

And she was bleeding again. He wet a fresh cloth and gave it to her.

You want anything? he said.

No. I don't want nothin.

He took down a knotted handkerchief from the sideboard and untied it, laying the cloth out and unfolding a small sheaf of paper dollars. He counted them and took one, together with what loose coins there were, and put these in the pocket of his overalls. Then he retied the kerchief with the remaining money and put it back in the cupboard.

I'm gone, he said.

All right.

He stopped at the door and looked at her. She turned her head away slowly.

It was midmorning when he set out and it took him just a little over an hour to reach the store at the junction, the sun warm on his back and the fine pumice of the road already paling and going to dust again. A horsefly followed behind his head as if towed there on a string.

When he got to the store it was closed. He rattled the latch and peered inside. From an upper window a voice called down: We still christians here. You'll have to come back a weekday. He turned away. By noon he was at the cabin again, sitting on a stump in the glade and carving at it intently with his knife. When he went in she was asleep in her foul bed. He sat before the fireplace watching ashes rise and wheel feebly in the cold light that fell there. She stirred heavily in her sleep, moaning. He watched her. When he could stay no longer he went out again and walked on the road. He could not decide what to do. He sat on a stone by the side of the road and with a dead stick drew outlandish symbols in the dust.

They made their meal that night on the last stale pieces of cornbread, a fine mold like powdered jade beginning on them where they lay dried and curling in the cupboard. She did not even ask him about the store. After she was asleep he again appropriated the quilt from off the bed and spread it upon the floor. He removed his shoes and lay down and folded the quilt over himself and stared at what shadows the joists and beams made upon the roof's underside. The lamp guttered and ceased. His eyes were closed. Before he slept he saw again the birth-stunned face, the swamp trees in a dark bower above the pale and naked flesh and the black blood seeping from the navel.

He woke early, the hard boarding laminated against his spine. A smoky light crept on the one pane of glass. He rose and refolded the quilt, replaced it at the foot of the bed and got his shoes and put them on, watching her, finally leaning above her wasted face to hear her breath. He took a drink of water from the bucket and opened the door on this new day, leaning in the doorframe, drinking. He shook the last of the water from the dipper and stretched, one hand to the small of his back.

Before it was full daylight he had gone to the spring again, the empty pail jiggling against his thigh, against pathside briers with a tin squeal, kneeling finally and watching the water suck cold and sandy over the bucket rim, filling and setting it on the bank and laving water on his wrists and forearms, dipping two palmfuls against his forehead, leaning his mouth into the meniscal calm of it, wide and tilting in the water the eyes that watched his eyes.

He set the bucket on the table and took up the weightless dipper and floated it on top. She was watching him.

I'd admire to have me a drink of that there fresh spring-water, she said.

He brought it to her, watched her drink.

You want more? he said.

She held up the empty dipper. If they is some, she said.

They's a bucketful if you want it.

She sat with her hands clasped between her breast and her belly while he brought the dipper to her again. Light from the window lay in a niggardly stain across the bed.

If that old winder was warshed, she said, I bet you could see out ever which way.

Funny to me you never noticed it when you was up and able.

I could get out my own self then, she said. Stead of havin to lay up and look out a winder.

He took the empty dipper from her and crossed the room.

I ain't warshin no winders, he said.

Well.

Well what?

Nothin. I just said well.

You better just.

I thought I heard that old tinker back this mornin, she said. Messin around.

He had been looking through the cupboard and now he stopped and closed the doors and looked at her. She was staring vacantly out toward the pines. That old tinker, he said, is long gone.

She looked at him. I just wondered, she said. I heard some kind of commotion sounded like him.

Well it wasn't.

She watched him. Where you goin? she said.

Store.

You reckon they got ary bit more of that black candy like they had?

I'll see, he said.

All right.

Don't take in no strangers while I'm gone.

She sighed deeply. They ain't a soul in this world but what is a stranger to me, she said.

She was keeping tally of the days. At the end of a week she climbed from the bed and walked to the foot of it and back. The next day she couldn't get up at all. But within the week she was walking about the cabin painfully each time he left.

One evening when he came in she was sitting in the chair, demurely and half-smiling, her figure thin and wasted under the ragged shift she wore as if great age had come upon her and her eyes huge and fever-black. He entered slowly and shut the door. Well, he said. You feelin that peart?

I'm better from what I was.

You've fell off considerable, ain't ye?

Lord, she said, I've gained back from what I was. I was puny as . . . I wasn't nothin but a shadder.

He eased himself down on the bed. When he looked at her again and the light falling slantwise across her he could see like dark tears two milkstains in the thin cotton cloth. He looked away. His hands lay palmupward on his thighs and he sat watching them as if they were somehow unaccountable.

Within the next few days she was walking about in the dooryard, taking the sun, as she said. He watched her poke along in her mincing shuffle, as if she carried an egg between her knees. Mend, woman, he said. He was sitting crosslegged in the shade of the house with the shotgun dismantled and hammering at the worn searnotch with a piece of wagon spring.

You fixin to tear up daddy's gun, she said.

It ain't daddy's gun, he said, not looking up.

She watched him. You ain't got ary shells, she said.

He held the lockplate between his knees and cocked the hammer. Now damn ye, slip if ye can, he said.

What? she said.

I was talkin to the gun.

Culla, she said.

What.

Nothin.

But two days later she stopped him as he came through the door with the chipped and yellowed pail in which he bore water, her standing almost in the doorway and arresting him with one arm. He paused to lean against the jamb and looked down at her. Well, he said, what?

Culla . . .

He went past her and put the bucket on the table. She had her hand to her mouth, watching him with huge eyes. He put the dipper in the pail and took a drink. He wiped his mouth and looked at her.

Culla . . .

What, damn it.

I just wanted to ast where it's at.

He winced and his eyes went narrow. What do you mean? he said.

Her hands worked nervously. I just wanted to know where it was you put him . . .

In the ground.

Well, she said, I just thought maybe if you was to show me where at I could see it . . . and maybe put some flowers or somethin . . .

Flowers, he said. It ain't even got a name.

She was twisting her hands again and he came from the table where he had been leaning and started past her.

Culla . . .

He stopped at the door and looked at her. She hadn't even looked around.

We could give it one, she said.

It's dead, he said. You don't name things dead.

She turned slowly. It wouldn't hurt nothin, she said.

Damn you, he said. The flowers if you want. I'll show ye.

He crossed the clearing in the windy sunlight, unmindful of her hobbling behind him, stopping at the edge of the woods where the path went until she should catch up, not even turning to watch this child's figure that struggled toward him like a crippled marionette. He pointed out the way to her. To the footlog, he said. Then you want to go right. They's a clearin, a clump of blackhaws. You'll see it.

She went happily, flushed, shuffling through the woods and plucking the shy wildflowers that sat upon the sunpatched earth and half shrouded under old leaves glared back a small violence of color upon the bland March skies. With her bouquet clutched in both hands before her she stepped finally into the clearing, a swatch of grass, sunlight, birdcalls, crossing with quiet and guileless rectitude to stand before a patch of black and cloven earth.

Some willingness to disbelief must have made her see and reflect. Certainly it could have held a grown man, this piece of ground gutted and strewn with mulch, slugwhite roots upturned to the disastrous light. She bent slowly and with pain and laid the flowers down. She knelt so for some time, and then she leaned forward and placed one palm on the cool earth. And then she began to scoop away the dirt with her hands.

She had not dug but a few inches before she came upon packed clay, unsevered roots. She chose another spot and soon uncovered a bedded rock which bared to the oblique lightfall of the sun's retrograde lay scored with powdery axemarks.

His long shadow overrode her but she did not see it. She stood and turned and found herself against his chest. She screamed and fell back, stumbled to the ground crushing the flowers, the blood starting again, warm on her leg. But he was the one: kneeling in the dark earth with his writhen face howling at her, saying Now you done it. Now you really went and done it. And her own face still bland and impervious in such wonder he mistook for accusation, silent and inarguable female invective, until he rose and fled, bearing his clenched hands above him threatful, supplicant, to the mute and windy heavens.

THEY ENTERED the lot at a slow jog, the peaceful and ruminative stock coming erect, watchful, shifting with eyes sidled as they passed, the three of them paying no heed, seeming blind with purpose, passing through an ether of smartweed and stale ammonia steaming from the sun-bleared chickenrun and on through the open doors of the barn and almost instantly out the other side marvelously armed with crude agrarian weapons, spade and brush-hook, emerging in an explosion of guineafowl and one screaming sow, unaltered in gait demeanor or speed, parodic figures transposed live and intact and violent out of a proletarian mural and set mobile upon the empty fields, advancing against the twilight, the droning bees and windtilted clover.

THE STORM had abated but rain still fell. He sat watching it with his chin propped on the soured and thinworn knees of his overalls, crouched on his narrow strip of dead earth, the fine clay dust musty and airless even above the rank breath of the wet spring woods. Night came and he slept. When he woke again it was to such darkness he did not trust his balance. He was very cold. He curled himself up on the ground and listened to the rain drifting in a rapid patter with the wind across the forest. When morning came he was sitting again with his knees tucked up, waiting, and with the first smoky portent of light he rose and set forth from the shelter of the cliff and through the steaming woods to the road, now a flume of ashcolored loam through which he struggled with weighted shoes, his hands pocketed and head cupped between his shoulderblades.

He reached the town before noon, mud slathered to his knees, wading through a thick mire in which the tracks of wagons crossed everywhere with channels of milky gray water, entering the square among the midday traffic, a wagon passing him in four pinwheels of flickering mud. He watched it pull up before a store, the horse coming to rest in an ooze that reached its fetlocks and the high wheels of the wagon sucking halfway to their hubs. He reached the store as the driver was turning and getting down. Howdy, he said.

How do, said the driver, pulling a sack from the wagon bed. A mite boggy, ain't she?

Yes tis, he said. You need any help?

Thank ye, said the man. I can get it all right.

He levered the sack onto his shoulder, nodded to Holme standing there holding the door, and went in, disappearing to the rear of the building. Holme approached the counter, unknotting the kerchief and removing two coins.

Yes, the clerk said, looking up out of the shabby and ludicrous propriety of his celluloid collar and winecolored cravat, his slight figure lost in a huge green coat coarsewoven and yieldless as iron.

Dime's worth of cheese and crackers, Holme said.

A dime's worth each?

No, both.

A nickel's worth each then, the clerk said.

Holme was looking about him at the varieties of merchandise. He looked at the clerk. What? he said.

I said a nickel's worth each.

That'd be a sight of crackers wouldn't it?

I don't know.

Holme seemed to be thinking about something else. After a minute he drummed his knuckles on the counter and looked up. You ever eat cheese and crackers? he said.

Yes, said the clerk with dignity.

Well, I'd like a dime's worth like a person would eat.

The clerk adjusted the shoulders of his weighty coat with a shrug and went down the counter to where a wooden box stood and from which he began to ladle crackers into a paper. Then he went on, stooping below the counter. Holme wasn't watching. His gray eyes moved over the tiered wares with vague wonder.

The clerk returned and laid the cheese and crackers before him each wrapped in a paper and looked up at him. What else now, he said.

Take out for a dope, Holme said, nudging the coins across the tradeworn wood.

To drink here?

Just outside.

You like two pennies, the clerk said with a small malignant smile.

For what?

The bottle.

I ain't going but just to the front stoop with it.

Well, he don't like for me to let em leave the store.

Holme looked at him.

Course if you ain't got it you could drink it in here.

Shit, Holme said.

The clerk flushed. Holme reached again into the pocket of his overalls and plucked forth the kerchief. He took out the two bits of copper with a disdainful flourish and let them trickle down over the counter.

Thank ye, said the clerk, raking the coins into his palm.

He rattled them into the wooden cashdrawer and looked up at Holme with satisfaction.

Holme grunted, gathered up the two packets, crossed the floor to the coolbox and got the drink and went out. While he was sitting on the stone veranda eating the cheese and crackers in the noon sun the wagon driver reappeared from the store and took a practiced leap up onto the box, unlooped the reins from the whipstand and cocked one mudcumbered boot upon the dashboard.

Say, Holme said.

The driver paused in the act of chucking the reins and looked down. Yes, he said.

Say you don't need no help?

No, don't believe I do.

Well, you don't know where a man might find work hereabouts do ye?

The driver studied him. Him looking up with eyes narrowed against the light, his jaws working slowly over the dry crackers.

Steady work?

Any kind.

Well, the driver said. The mill ort to be takin on summer hands in a week or so. He looked down at the man again but the man said nothing, watching him, chewing. Yes, he said. Listen. Maybe the squire might have somethin. Some work around the house or somethin. He seized up the reins again.

Where's he at?

The man took the reins in one hand and with the other he pointed down the road to the north. Bout a quarter mile, he said. Big house on the left as you leave town. You'll see it. He lifted the reins and chucked them and the horse leaned into the traces and broke the wheels with a slight sucking noise.

Much obliged, Holme said.

The man raised one hand.

He watched them go, the bottle tilted upward to his mouth, watching the horse veer and wobble, the wheels dripping back into their furrows the upturned clots of muck. He took the empty bottle inside and collected his money and came out again and started down the road the way the man had directed him.

He did see it, a large two-storey house fronted with wooden columns on which the paint lay open in long fents like slashed paper and a yellow stain of road dust paling upward in the sunlight until the gables shone clean and white. He turned up the graveled drive and walked around the house, along a little cobbled walkway until he came to what he took for the back door. He tapped and waited. No one came. He tapped again. After a while he went on to the other side of the house. There was a kitchen door and a window through which he could see an old negro woman bending over a table and paring potatoes. He tapped at the glass.

She came to the door and opened it and looked at him.

Is the squire in? he said.

Just a minute, she said, pushing the door half to but not closing it. He could hear her shuffling away and then he could hear her calling. He waited. Presently he heard bootsteps crossing the floor and then the door opened again and a big man looked out at him with hard black eyes and said Yes.

Howdy, he said. I was talkin to a man down to the store said you might need some help. Said you might have some work . . .

No, the squire said.

Well, he said. I thank ye. He turned and started away.

You, the squire said.

He stopped and looked back.

You don't mind no for a answer, do ye?

I figured you would know one way or the other, he said.

Or maybe you don't need work all that bad.

I ast for it. I ain't scared to . . .

Come here a minute.

He retraced his steps and stood facing the squire again, the squire looking him over with those hard little eyes as he would anything for sale. You got a good arm, he said. Can you swing a axe?

I've been knowed to, he said.

The squire seemed to weigh something in his mind. Tell you what I'll do with you, he said. You want to earn your supper they's a tree blowed down out back here needs cut up to stovewood.

All right.

All right, eh? Wait here a minute. He went away in the house and then in a few minutes he was back and led the man outside, motioning him with one finger across the yard toward a workshed. They entered and he could see in the gloom a negro bent over a piece of machinery.

John, the squire said.

The negro rose wordlessly and approached them.

Give this man a axe, he said. He turned to Holme. Can you sharp it?

Yessir, he said.

And turn the wheel for him to sharp it.

The negro nodded. Right, said the squire. Ever man to grind his own axe. All right. It's in the side over yander. You'll see it. Just a little old pine. What's your name?

Holme.

You ain't got but one name?

Culla Holme.

What?

Culla.

All right, Holme. I like to know a man's name when I hire him. I like to know that first. The rest I can figure for myself. John here will fix you up. Two-foot chunks and holler when you get done.

He went out and Holme was left facing the negro. The negro had yet to speak. He went past with a great display of effort, one hand to his kidney, shuffling. He fumbled in a corner of the shed for some time and came forth with the axe from the clutter of tools in a broken barrel. The man watched him take it up with endless patience out of a shapeless bloom of staves skewed all awry as if this container had been uncoopered violently in some old explosion, take it up and hand it to him without comment and shuffle on to the stone which he now began to crank. Holme watched him. The wheel trundled woodenly. He laid the rusted bit against it and pressed out a sheaf of sparks which furled in a bright orbit there and raced and faded across the negro's glistening face, a mute black skull immune to fire, the eyes closed, a dark wood carving provoked again and again out of the gloom until the steel was properly sharp.

That's good, he said.

The negro opened his eyes, rose and nodded and returned to the bench where he had been working. He went out, hefting the weight of the axe in his hand and by the better light at the door of the shed examining the edge of it.

The tree was not far from the house. It was broken off some six feet from the ground and the standing trunk with its hackle of ribboned wood looked like it had been chewed off by some mammoth browsing creature. He paced off the fallen section and straddling the trunk, working backwards, dressed off the limbs. Then he marked off two feet from the butt end and sank the axe into the wood.

He worked easily, letting the weight of the axehead carry the bite. He had cut four sections before he stopped to rest. He looked at what he was doing and then he looked at the sun. He stood the axe against the stump and returned to the shed to look for the negro but he wasn't there. He crossed the yard to the kitchen door again and knocked. When she opened it he could smell cooking. I wonder could I see the squire a minute, he said.

The squire came to the door and peered out at him as if dim of recollection. What? he said. A saw? I thought you was done.

No sir, not yet. I thought maybe it might go a little quicker with a saw.

The squire watched him as if awaiting some further explanation. Holme looked down at his feet. Across the doorsill in the rich aura of cookery the squire's figure reared silently out of a pair of new veal boots.

Just a little old bucksaw or somethin, Holme said.

They ain't no saw, the squire said. It's broke.

Well.

I thought you hired out as a axe-hand.

Holme looked up at him.

Wasn't that what you hired out for?

Yessir, Holme said. I reckon. He looked at the squire to see if he might be smiling but the squire wasn't smiling.

Was there anything else you wanted?

No sir. I reckon not.

Well.

Well, Holme said. I'll get on back to it.

The squire said nothing. Holme turned and started back across the yard. As he passed through the gate he looked back. The squire had not moved. He stood rigid and upright in the coffin-sized doorway with no expression, no hint of a smile, no list to his bearing.

He worked on through the afternoon while shadow of post and tree drew lean and black across the grass. It was full evening before he was done. He stacked the last pieces and shouldered the axe and went on across the lot toward the shed. This time the negro was there and he handed him the axe, still neither of them speaking, and went to the door of the house again and knocked for the third time this day.

I won't even ast if you're done, the squire said.

All right.

All right. Well. I reckon you're hungry ain't ye?

Some.

I reckon you just eat twice a day. Or is it once?

Why? Holme said.

You never ate no dinner as I know of.

I wasn't offered none.

You never ast for none.

Holme was silent.

You never ast for nothin.

I just come huntin work, Holme said.

The squire hauled by its long chain a watch from somewhere in his coat, snapped it open and glanced at it and put it away. It's near six o'clock, he said. Likin about three minutes. How much time would you say you put in on that job?

I don't know, Holme said. I don't know what time it was I commenced.

Is that right? Don't know?

No sir.

Well it was just before dinner. And now it's just before supper. That's the best part of half a day. Ain't it?

I reckon, he said.

The squire leaned slightly forward. For your supper? he said.

Holme was silent.

So I reckon a full day would be for dinner and supper. Still ain't said nothin about breakfast. Let alone a place to sleep. Not even to mention money.

You was the one, Holme said. You said what . . .

And you was the one said all right. Come on man. What is it you've done. Where are you runnin from? Heh?

I ain't runnin from nowheres.

No? You ain't? Where you from? I never ast you that, did I?

I come from down on the Chicken River.

No, the squire said. My wife's people was from down thataway little as I like to say it.

I just lived there this past little while. I never claimed to of been borned there.

Before that then. Where did you live before?

I come from downstate.

I bet you do at that, the squire said. And then you come up here. Or down in Johnson County. And now you up here. What is it? You like to travel? When did you eat last if it's any of my business.

I et this mornin.

This mornin. Out of somebody's garden most likely.

I got money, Holme said.

I won't ast ye where you come by it. You married?

No. I ain't married. He looked up at the squire. Their shadows canted upon the whitewashed brick of the kitchen shed in a pantomime of static violence in which the squire reeled backward and he leaned upon him in headlong assault. It ain't no crime to be poor, he said.

No, it ain't. It ain't a crime. I hope you've not got a family. It's a sacred thing, a family. A sacred obligation. Afore God.

The squire had been looking away and now he turned to Holme again. It ain't no crime to be poor, he said. That's right. But shiftlessness is a sin, I would judge. Wouldn't you?

I reckon, he said.

Yes. The bible reckons. What I got I earned. They's not a man in this county will tell ye different. I've never knowed nothin but hard work. I've been many a time in the field at daybreak waitin for the sun to come up to commence work and I was there when it went down again. Daybreak to backbreak for a Godgiven dollar. They ain't a man in this county will dispute it.

Holme was looking down, one hand crossed over the back of the other the way men stand in church. There was a commotion of hens from beyond the barn, a hog's squeal, ceasing again into the tranquillity of birdcalls and cicadas.

All right, Holme, the squire said. I ain't goin to ast you no more of your business. He had out a small leather purse now which he unsnapped and lightened by the weight of a half-dollar. Here, he said. And your supper. Supper's at six-thirty. In the kitchen. You can wash up now if you've a mind to.

He took the coin, holding it in his hand as if he had no place to put it. All right, he said.

After he had washed he sat in the shade of the toolshed and pared idly at the sole of his shoe with the knife he carried. He watched the negro cross from the barn to the house. In a few minutes he came from the kitchen door and returned across the yard again, a small figure scuttling from shadow to shadow with laborious ill-grace, carrying in one hand the squire's boots and disappearing into the barn.

The squire was an early riser and it was not yet good light when he went to the barn. You Holme, he called up the chaffdusted ladder and into the dark hatchway of the loft. No one answered. The negro was coming through the far end of the barn carrying a bucket.

Where's he at, the squire said. Is he gone?

The negro nodded his head.

He sure is a early bird. When did he skedaddle?

The negro slid the bucket up onto his wrist and made a motion with his hands.

Well, the squire said. He looked about him uncertainly, like a man who has forgotten something. Then he said: Where's them boots?

The negro had started toward the corncrib and now he stopped and looked around, his face already shining with grease or sweat, whatever it was, like wet obsidian. He did not even motion with his hands. They stood looking at each other for just a minute and then the squire said Goddamn. I will be purely goddamned. That ingrate son of a bitch. You never should of left . . . Hitch up for me while I get the shotgun. Turning and wheeling out of the barn, the negro following him with that same poverty of motion and taking up harness gear from where it hung on the wall as he went. In a few minutes the squire was back with the shotgun and a white hat jammed onto his head, leaping up into the wagon and sitting there in furious immobility and then leaping down again to fumble with the harness while the negro led the horse forth from the stall, not telling him to hurry or anything so useless and finally waiting in a throb of violent constraint while the negro backed the horse between the wagon shafts and while he hitched it and until he stepped back and then raising up the reins and slapping them across the horse's rump, lifting two ribbons of rank dust out of its hide and starting and then as suddenly drawing up again and leaning down:

Town? You think he might of gone back through . . . No. All right, I'll—the mute negro laboring in the air with his dark and boney fingers and the squire: The what? The brush-hook? What else? Damn. Goddamn. —and exploding out of the lot with the horse rearing under the reins and the wagon skewing about and then down the drive onto the road at a mad clatter and gone.

The negro returned to the barn and took up the pail from where he had left it, going past the stalls to the corncrib where he seated himself on a milking stool and began to shell corn, his hard hand twisting the kernels loose and them sifting bright and hard down into the pail, ringing like coins.

The squire at midmorning was following a log road, urging the horse on and the horse already faded to a walk, when they came out of the brush behind him. He turned when he heard them and he turned back. They were coming along the road. One of them said something and then one of them said Harmon and then one of them was alongside seizing the horse's reins. The squire stood in the wagon. Here, he said. What do you think you're doing. Here now, by God—reaching and taking up the shotgun where it stood leaning against the seat.

THEY CAME across the field attended by a constant circus of grasshoppers catapulting from the sedge and entered the wood deployed in the same ragged phalanx while before them passed solitary over no visible road a horse and a wagon surmounted by a harriedlooking man in a white hat. They altered their course and came upon a log road down which the wagon receded in two thin tracks and upon a burst lizard who dragged his small blue bowels through the dirt, breaking into a trot, a run, the first of them reaching the horse and seizing the reins and turning up to the driver a mindless smile, clutching the horse's withers and clinging there like some small and vicious anthroparian and the driver rising in remonstration from the wagon box so that when the next one came up behind him sideways in a sort of dance and swung the brush-hook it missed his neck and took him in the small of the back severing his spine and when he fell he fell unhinged sideways and without a cry.

SHE DID NOT KNOW that he had taken the gun. She did not know that the money was gone and she had never known how much there was of it. She went about the house gathering her things, laying out her dress on the bed and examining it before she stripped out of the shift and put it on. She pirouetted slowly in the center of the room like a doll unwinding for just a moment and then took off the dress and scrubbed herself with a rag and cold water as best she could and with a piece of broken comb raked her dead yellow hair. She set out her shoes and dusted them and put them on, and the dress. Of the shift she made a package in which lay rolled her small and derelict possessions and thus equipped she took a final look about to see what had been forgotten. There was nothing. She tucked the package beneath her arm and set forth, shortgaited and stiffly, humming softly to herself and so into the sunshine that washed fitfully with the spring wind over the glade, turning her face up to the sky and bestowing upon it a smile all bland and burdenless as a child's.

She crossed the river bridge, walking carefully on the

illfitted planks, looking down at the water. She nudged pebbles through the cracks and watched them diminish with slow turnings into sudden printed rings upon the river that sucked away like smoke. She went on, resting from time to time quietly by the side of the road and patting the sweat from her brow with the parcel she carried. When she came at last into sight of the crossroads she could see someone coming far down the road and misshapen with heat. She looked about her and then entered the pine woods to her left and climbed a small rise which commanded the road. It was very warm. She sat fanning herself and the gnats that shimmered before her eyes. It was an old woman who came along laden with empty mealsacks and conversing earnestly with herself. Later two boys passed laughing and punching each other. The watcher on the hill fanned and sighed. I wisht he'd come on, she said.

When he did come he looked like a man who has a long way to go. He had the supplies in a sack over his shoulder and he went by slowly with his eyes to the ground. She crouched low while he passed and when he was gone she rose and dusted off her dress and took up her bundle and returned to the road again, walking out his tracks to the crossroads and the store.

The storekeeper was a dark lean German of middle years whose wry humor merely puzzled the occupants of the five hundred square miles of sparse and bitter land he commissaried. He watched her at the screen door until she got it open and entered, diffident, almost disdainful, as if sore put upon to take her trade to such a place.

How do, he said.

When she looked at him he saw that she must have been ill, her eyes huge and sunken in her pallid face and the dress slack and folded upon her. She nodded gravely. I wonder could I get a drink of water from ye, she said.

Yes mam. He came from behind the counter, noticing now the bundle of cloth she carried so darkened with sweat and her way with it as if she would keep it from sight. He crossed the dark oiled floor to the box and drew up the waterjar, loosed the tin screwcap for her and handed it across. She took it in both hands and thanked him and tilted a long drink down her thin throat.

Get all ye want, he said. Just set it back when you're done.

Thank ye, she said, holding the jar before her and getting her breath before she drank again.

Been a little warmer ain't it? Today.

She arrested the jar at her mouth and lowered it and said Lord ain't it been, then raised the jar and drank some more. When she was done she replaced the cap and put the jar back in the cooling box.

Was they anything else for ye?

I thank ye, she said, I believe that's all. What do I owe ye?

That's all right, he said.

Well I thank ye.

Yes. Have ye got far to go?

Where to?

There was a moment of silence. The storekeeper tugged at one ear. Well, he said, I don't know. I allowed you was travelin.

I hope not to have to a whole lot, she said. I'm a-huntin that tinker is what it is.

Tinker?

That'n come thew here about two weeks ago they said never had no cocoa.

The storekeeper waited for her to continue. She was looking up at him curiously. She said: Have you not seen him?

He shook his head slowly. No, he said.

It wasn't but about two weeks ago.

No, he said. I've not seen him.

Had just the littlest chap with him.

Tinkers don't stop here, the storekeeper said, and I don't welcome em to. They has most likely been one thew here lately. I don't know. They come and go. But they ain't lookin for me and I sure ain't lookin for them.

Well, I thank ye.

And I ain't got no cocoa neither.

I know it, she said. My brother trades here.

Brother?

Yessir. I expect you know him.

I expect I do if he trades here. What's his name?

He's in here this afternoon. Culla Holme.

Why he just left here. Quiet feller? Come in here this afternoon with that old shotgun and sold it to Buddy Sizemore?

He done that? she said.

Well, the storekeeper said, maybe I ought not to of told that.

I'd hate for you to know what all else he done, she said.

The storekeeper started to smile and then he stopped smiling. She hitched the bundle up beneath her arm and cast about her with her sunken eyes. I thank ye for the water, she said.

Yes, he said. You welcome.

Well. I best get on.

Come back, he said.

At the door she stopped again, turned, trapped in fans of dusty light, a small black figure burning. Listen, she said.

Yes.

I'd take it as a favor if you'd not tell him I been in here.

Your brother.

Yessir. Him or that tinker either one.

She stood for a while on the porch, the shadows long upon the road and the birds growing quiet. She looked to her left and to her right, the sandy pike coming out of the forest and flaring at the store and going on again. She crossed the road and turned to face the store for a moment and then she started up the road to the left. She walked very slowly. Before she had gone two miles she was walking in darkness. A cool wind came out of the forest. From time to time she stopped and listened but there was nothing to hear. She heard her steps small and faint in the silence. When she saw the light through the trees before her she stopped again, warily, her hands to her labored heart.

She was met at the door of this small house by a man holding aloft a lantern beyond which and gathered in its fringe of wan light she could see the faces of several women of different ages, including an ancient crone who was without a nose.

Yes, the man said. What is it?

The old woman's black eyes closed and opened again slowly on either side of such long bat's nostrils.

Are ye lost?

She clutched up her bundle. Lost, she said. Yes, I'm lost. I wondered could I just rest a spell.

The man watched her, one hand raised with the lantern, the other fondling a button at his chest.

Yes. Tell her yes.

Thank ye, she said.

The man turned to the woman who had spoken. Hush, he said. He turned again to the traveler. Where do ye come from now?

Just down the road a piece. I just wondered could I maybe rest a little spell.

Just a piece down the road? Must be a considerable piece for me not to know ye. You live twards town?

I don't know, she said.

Ha, the man said, don't know where ye live?

I mean I don't know where town's at.

The man's eyes grew narrow. Who's out there with you? he said.

They ain't nobody but me. I'm just by myself.

Who's out there? he called, looking past her and addressing the untenanted night out of which she had come.

She turned and looked with him.

Come up, whoever's out there.

These faces watched but no one appeared. The man turned to her. You sure they ain't nobody with ye?

No, she said. I just come by myself.

All right. Which way did ye come?

I live down twards the Chicken River.

Say ye do? And where is it you're headed on such a dark night,

I'm a-huntin this here tinker.

Tinker? What'd he steal?

Well. Somethin belonged to me.

And what was that?

It was just somethin.

Well come in anyway.

Thank ye, she said.

The women parted before them and they advanced upon and set back the darkness inside as far as a large trestle table where the man turned and put down the lamp. Now, he said. This here is my family. They's a boy here somewheres. Where's he at, old woman?

He had better be bringin me in some wood.

He's a-bringin in wood. Now, what was your name young woman?

Rinthy Holme.

All right. This here's the family. Dinner be ready here in just a few minutes. Ain't that right?

The woman nodded.

And you welcome.

Thank ye, she said. She turned to the woman but she had

already gone from the room. The grandmother and two girls or women of some age stood watching her.

Get ye a chair, the man said.

They watched her sit, holding the bundle up before her, the lamp just at her elbow belabored by a moth whose dark shape cast upon her face appeared captive within the delicate skull, the thin and roselit bone, like something kept in a china mask. Lord, she said, I've not sat hardly today.

They had been eating for several minutes before the boy joined them. He studied her with cadaverous eyes and began to load his plate. She reached another piece of the store bread from its wrapper. She said: I bet I ain't eat two pones of lightbread in my life. I was raised hard.

The woman regarded her above a poised and dripping forkful of fatmeat. We eat what we've a mind to here, she said. We ain't never had nothin but we don't care to get just whatever to eat if we got the money. Do we, Luther?

That's right, he said. I ain't never belittled my family nothin to eat they wanted. They get that baloney down at the store all the time. They can get them salmons if they've a mind to.

She nodded, holding the bread in one hand and applying the butter more slowly. They ate on in silence, jaws working all down the table with great sobriety, all sitting upright and formal saving the toothless old woman who bent nearsightedly into her plate with smacking gums, a sparse tuft of long white chin hairs wagging and drifting above the food.

When the man had finished he pushed back his plate and sat looking about at the others until they began to eat faster, finishing and looking up one by one until all were done but the grandmother. When she finished she set back her plate with one thumb and stared fixedly at the spot where it had been. The man reached and turned down the lamp until the flame showed but crosswise in the wickslot, a dull bronze heat quaking deep in the glass toward which their faces seemed to lean disembodied in a perimeter of smoking icons. The old woman's leathered lids had closed and she rocked slightly with the ebb of her dreams. Well, said the man, that's done with, and pushing back his chair he rose from the table. The women began to clear the dishes away, again saving the old woman who opened one eye and looked about and closed it again softly and secretive.

We goin to get a early start of the mornin, the man said.

If you can get that boy prised loose from the bed we might get out of here by midmornin, the woman said. She was wiping off the table. Wake up, mamma, fore ye fall out of the chair again.

That boy'll be up. Won't ye, Bud? Where's he at?

If the waterbucket or woodbox is either one empty he'll be beyond earshout for sure. Here honey, give me them and set down and rest.

She held the plates stacked against her breast. It's all right, she said. I don't care to help.

Well mind the step yander.

All right. I got to get on directly anyhow.

You ain't goin nowheres tonight.

Well, she said.

Just mind the step yander.

When they had done in the kitchen she followed the woman down the passageway at the rear of the house, the woman holding the lamp before them and so out into the cool night air and across the boardfloored dogtrot, the door falling to behind them and the woman opening the next one and entering, her close behind, a whippoorwill calling from nearby for just as long as they passed through the open and hushing instantly with the door's closing. She stopped alongside the woman, looking about at the room in which they stood, the two beds that met headfirst in the far corner, one brass and cheaply ornate and the other plain oak, the washstand between them with a porcelained tin basin and a pitcher. The woman set the lamp upon a narrow shelf nailed to the wall.

You want to warsh they's soap yander. They's a pitcher of water at the well if it needs primed.

I thank ye, she said, holding the rolled clothes to her breast yet.

When ye get done and get abed just blow out the lamp. Take the big bed yander.

All right.

The woman had started to turn back and now she stopped at the door, eyes squinting and oblique to the light half-masked and narrow as a cat's. Was they anything you needed? she said.

The young woman looked down, fidgeting with the bundle. No, she said. I ain't needin nothin. I thank ye.

Well, the woman said. She opened the door and the night air came upon them again sweetly through the warm reek of the room, the whippoorwill calling more distant, the door closing and the woman's steps fading across the dogtrot and the bird once again more faintly, or perhaps another bird, beyond the warped and waney boards and thin yellow flame that kept her from the night.

She laid her bundle down on the bed and took the lamp and the basin and soap and went out, holding the lamp votively before her and the heat rising pleasantly about her face. She watched the ground, going with care, the basin upright and riding her hip, slowly, processional, a lone acolyte passing across the barren yard, face seized in the light she bore. She found the well and set the basin on the stone pumpstand, adjusted it beneath the spout, took up the long handle and began to work it. It gave out a hoarse gasp and then she felt the long pull of water in the pipe, rising, glutting the iron mouth and spilling into the basin. She took the soap and lathered her hands up in a gritty curded paste, spreading it over her face and then dashing cold water after it, eyes shut fiercely against the soap's caustic sting. When she had finished she rinsed the basin and took up the lamp from the ground and started for the house. The whippoorwill had stopped and she bore with her now in frenzied colliding orbits about the lamp chimney a horde of moths and night insects. Before she reached the steps she heard the rattle of his canvas breeches along the side of the house. Had she not had the lamp she could have seen him where he stood in the deeper shadow of the eaves watching her. She was upon the steps when he spoke.

Hidy, he said.

She paused and he entered the ring of light with such painful diffidence any watcher would have said he was about something of which he did not approve.

What is it? she said.

He stopped a few feet from her, his hands deep in the rear pockets of his trousers, scraping his feet on the ground like a man who has stepped in manure. Why, he said, I just seen ye goin in, thought I'd say hidy. Where ye goin?

Goin in.

Well, he said. Best not be in no hurry. He looked up at her, face tilted sideways and absurdly coy.

Well, she said, I reckon I best. I'm about give out.

He removed his hands from his pockets, locked his fingers and pushed them out before him until the knuckles cracked, raised them over his head and gripped the back of his neck with them. Kindly a pretty evenin, ain't it? he said.

She looked up at a sky heavy and starless above them and laden with the false warmth of impending storm. It's right dark, she said.

Now it is that, he said. Yes. It is a dark'n. He was looking all about him as if to see was it darker in some places than in others. You ain't afeard of the dark are ye?

No, she said. I don't reckon.

Shoot, he said. I bet you're afeard of the dark. I bet you won't blow out that there lamp. And me standin right here.

She watched him.

If you was to get scared I'd be right here. Bet ye.

Watched him above the glassrimmed flame, him standing loose and smiling a little.

I ain't got no match to light it back with, she said.

Pshaw, I got matches. Go on. Let's see if ye will.

I got to get in, she said.

His mouth snapped shut like a turtle's but she was not there to see it nor the lamp to see it by, already mounting the hewn poplar steps soundlessly and still with her air of staid and canonical propriety, entering the house and turning slender and moth-besieged and closing the door.

She put the lamp on the shelf and sat on the bed. It was a shuck tick and collapsed slowly beneath her with a dry brittle sound and a breath of stale dust. She turned down the lamp and removed her dress and hung it over the brass bedpost. Then she unrolled the shift and put it on and crawled into the bed. She lay on her back very quietly for several minutes, her hands clasped above her stomach, feeling the slack flesh beneath her shift. Then she sat up and cupping her hand behind the lamp chimney blew out the light.

It was only a few minutes before they entered, stepping soft as thieves and whispering harshly to one another. She watched them with squint eyes, the man all but invisible standing not an arm's length from where she lay and going suddenly stark white against the darkness as he shed his overalls and poised in his underwear before mounting awkwardly bedward like a wounded ghost. When they were all turned in they lay in the hot silence and listened to one another breathing. She turned carefully on her rattling pallet. She listened for a bird or for a cricket. Something she might know in all that dark.

They set out in the morning with the first light, having breakfasted at the same long table on pork and biscuits in a pale gray murk up through which the steam from the food rose eerily. The women wore their Sunday clothes, bonnets laid to hand for the trip, again saving the old woman who was still shrouded in the same voluminous material, neither dress nor housecoat but simply undifferentiated cloth in which she went shapeless and unhampered, moving in an aura of faint musk, the dusty odor of aged female flesh impervious to dirt as stone is or clay. They carried chairs out and waited in the chill dewfall while the boy took them one by one and set them in the wagon bed, the husband on the seat slumped and silent with the reins slack in his fingers and the single mule drowsing in like attitude, lifting its feet heavily. The women climbed aboard the wagon and took their seats, sweeping their skirts from under them against wrinkling—even the old woman by long habit—and when they were set the boy leaped up onto the box alongside the man and the man raised his head and turned to look at them, the five women sitting about in the housechairs with folded hands, then raised and let fall the reins and said Come up, and they surged forth in a mounting clash and rattle and advanced upon the road.

She was wearing the dress again and the shoes, the shift rolled into the same bundle with her things inside and held primly in her lap. What time do ye figure us to get there? she said.

Late mornin, the woman said, if this here old mule don't die in the traces.

He looks to be a right substantial mule to me.

He's about like everthing else around here, the woman said wearily. Here. Did I show ye this here quilt?

No mam.

She began to unwrap a package of its muslin cover and unrolled part of a large piecework quilt. If I could get these here girls to quilt we'd of had two or three.

She bent forward to examine it. The boy had leaned over the back of the wagon seat to watch and comment.

Last one I sold I got three dollars for it, but it was a double weddin ring, the woman said.

Thisn's right pretty, she said.

The boy had pulled out the quilting and was turning it in his hand. I don't see why anybody would want to give three dollars for a old quilt, he said.

No, the woman said, because you cain't give it if you ain't got it. Here, don't black it to where nobody won't have it.

The boy let it fall disdainfully and she rewrapped it in the muslin.

It's tedious to piece one for one person by herself, she said.

Yes mam.

The two girls said nothing at all and did not appear to be

listening. The old woman had turned her chair partly sideways and rode peering into the passing wall of wet shrubbery as if she held camera with something that paced them in the black pine woods beyond. After a while she leaned precariously from the wagon bed and broke a small twig from a spicewood bush, held it to her nostrils a moment and then with her opaque orange thumbnail began to fray the end of it.

They rode on through the new green woods under the rising sun where wakerobins marked the roadway with their foiled wax spears, climbing, the man jiggling the reins across the mule's tattered withers, through a cutback and into brief sunlight where the old woman hooked her bonnet more forward on her head and peered sideways at the others like a cowled mandrill, her puckerstrung mouth working the snuff that lay in her lower lip, turning again, a jet of black spittle lancing without trajectory across the edge of the wagon and into the woods, descending, the man working the brake, the wagon creaking and sidling a little in loose gravel, onto the flatland again, fording a weedgrown branch where dead water rusted the stones and through a canebrake where myriad small birds flitted and rustled dryly like locusts.

She watched the wet wheeltracks behind them go from black to nothing in the sand, caressing the rolled shift in her lap. It's a likely place for varmints such a place as this, ain't it? she said.

The woman looked about them. Likely enough, she said.

The husband tottered on the box, sleeping. The grandmother sat leaning forward with elbows on her knees, her face visible to no one. They rode through the mounting heat of the summer morning in silence save for the periodic spat of the old woman's snuff and the constant wooden trundling of the wagon, a sound so labored and remorseless as should have spoken something more than mere progress upon the earth's surface.

There was a spring halfway to town where they stopped, the man halting the wagon in the road and the mule leaning his long nose into the water that crossed here and baring beneath the silt small bright stones, mauve and yellow, drinking and blowing peacefully in this jeweled ford. They got down stiffly from the wagon and entered the wood along a footpath until they came to a place where water issued straight up out of a piece of swampy ground and poured off through lush grass. The woman took with her the lunch pail, wetting the rag with which it was covered and replacing it with care, taking her turn to drink from the tin cup that was kept here upended on a nubbed pole.

That's fine water, the man said. Fine a water as they is in this county.

She took the cup from him and dipped it into the dark pool, raised it clear and drank. It was sweet and very cold. She passed it on to the old woman who adjusted the snuff pouched in her lip and turned the cup to drink from the back side of it. When they had all drunk the man put the cup back on the pole and they started back down the path, the old woman dabbing at her mouth with a handful of skirt.

She had fallen in last behind the two girls and she was surprised to hear footsteps behind her. When she turned the boy was coming along jauntily.

I thought you'd gone on, she said.

I was up in the woods. Hot ain't it?

It is right warm, she said, going on now along the narrow black path and him at her elbow awkwardly.

Grammaw I reckon looks right funny to you don't she?

I don't know, she said.

Still I bet she does. I'm used to her.

They went on.

Know how she done it?

Done what?

Lost her beak.

No, she said. I never studied it.

You'll swear I'm a-lyin to ye but a stovepipe done it she was puttin up. Fell and sliced her off slick as a frog's . . . as a frog's belly.

I declare, she said.

They were coming out on the road now and he hushed and there was still the mule with his muzzle in the ford, untethered full in the road, his ears dipping and folding.

I'd think that old mule'd founder, she said.

Shoot, he said. That old mule's got more sense than a . . . Shoot, he's got all kinds of sense.

At the wagon she waited while they helped the old woman aboard and then climbed up after her.

Don't a cool drink just set ye up though, the woman said.

There was a commotion to the front of the wagon. God-damn it to hell, the boy howled. They could see him curled in the road holding his knee in both hands but there had been no one looking to see him swing up to the high seat with one leap as the drivers did or to see him miss his hand-hold and crack his knee on the metal step in falling.

Lord God he's kilt hisself, the woman said.

He needs that mouth attended to, the old woman muttered from beneath her hood.

The man got down from the wagon wearing a look of martyred patience. He bent over the boy and forcibly removed his hands from his knee. The trousers were ripped in a small tricorner going dark with blood.

He's stove a hole in his kneecap, the man said. The boy was lying on his side grimacing in histrionic anguish, suffering the man to slide the breechleg tight up on his thigh in chance ligature and poke a dirty finger at the laceration.

Tain't bleedin much, he said. Just let me bind him—reaching to his hip and drawing forth in garish foliation a scarlet and blue bandana.

Don't use that, the woman said. You ain't got nary othern now. Here. She was bending and ripped loose a long strip of muslin from the bundled quilt in the floor of the wagon.

Give it here then, the man said, reaching backward with one hand. He propped the boy's knee in his lap, squatting in the road, took the cloth and wrapped it and tied it. The boy hobbled to his feet and inspected the job before easing the leg of his trousers down. They mounted to the box and the man chucked up the sleeping mule and they went on, the boy upright on the seat, pilloried and stoic, the man slumped and brooding, and behind them the five women prim and farcical on their housechairs.

It was near noon when they came into the town, the

mule's thinshod hoofs going suddenly loud on the banked cobbles up to the rail crossing, one clear steel ring of his shoe on the polished bar and down again and again muted and dull in the unpaved street along which stood tethered an assortment of rigs with mules or horses and alike only in their habitude of dust and age and patience, the man now guiding the mule toward them with small tugs at the rein until they veered beneath the shade of what scantleaved trees lined the mall there and came to rest.

Well, he said, we here.

She was first down, holding the bundle to her chest and extending a hand to the grandmother who rose and looked about with disapproval before taking up the amplitude of dress that hung before her, ignoring the hand, gripping the rim of the high rear wheel and coming down it backwards ladderwise and expertly, alighting in the road and brushing down her skirts again and glaring out from beneath her dark bonnet fearfully.

The man had the rope from the wagon and was casting about for something to tie it to. The two girls and the woman were coming down the other side. She adjusted her belongings and spoke to the man:

I sure do thank ye for the good supper and bed and the ride in and all.

You welcome, he said. We just fixin to take dinner now so don't be in no rush.

Well I best get on and get started.

You welcome to take dinner with us, the woman said.

I thank ye but I best get on.

Well. We'll be goin back early of the evenin if you want to ride with us.

I thank ye, she said, but I reckon I'll be goin on.

The man was tapping a loop of the rope in one hand. The woman was holding the quilt in her arms like a child. All right, the woman said, and the man said: Do you ever pass this way again just stay with us.

She entered the first store she came to and went straight down the cluttered aisle to the counter where a man stood waiting.

You seen that tinker? she said.

I beg your pardon?

You welcome. That tinker. He been thew here?

I don't know, the man said. I don't know what tinker it is you're talkin about.

Well, she said. It's just a old tinker. Have you seen ary tinkers a-tall come thew here.

Mam we got a better line here than any tinker carries and price is more reasonable too. Just what all was it you was interested in?

I ain't wantin to buy nothin. I'm just a-huntin this here tinker.

Well you won't find him in here.

You don't know where he might of got to or nothin?

I don't keep up with no tinkers. You might try Belkner's. Some of them stocks there I would reckon. They shoddy enough.

Where is it at?

Cross the street and up about five doors. Big sign, hardware.

I thank ye, she said.

You welcome.

The boy caught up with her crossing the street, limping fast and looking harried. Hold up a minute, he said. Listen.

She stopped and shaded her eyes against the sun.

I slipped off, he said. Listen, you want to go to that show tonight?

What show is that?

Some show they havin. I got money.

How you aim to get back home? Your folks ain't goin to lay over for no show.

That's all right, he said. I can get back. I'll tell em somethin. You want to go?

I cain't, she said.

How come?

I just cain't. I got some things I got to do.

You ain't no schoolteacher are ye?

No.

Well. Do you not hold with goin to shows?

I ain't never been to nary. I don't reckon they's nothin wrong with it.

He had his hands in the rear pockets of his canvas pants. In the powdered dust of the street he had created a small amphitheatre with the sole of one shoe. I don't see why ye cain't go, he said. You a widder didn't I hear ye say?

Yes.

Well. You ain't got ary beau have ye?

No, she said.

Well.

She watched him curiously. She had not taken her hand from above her eyes.

Well, I don't see why all ye cain't go.

I just cain't, she said.

Won't, he said.

No.

Looky here. He drew forth from his pocket a deep leather purse, the brass catches grown with a bilegreen crust. He coyly slid a sheaf of bills out and riffled them before her. She watched. She let her hand fall to the bundle at her breast, blinking in the sun. He worked the money. It's a bunch of it ain't it? he said. Bet you ain't never . . .

I got to go, she said.

Here, wait up a minute.

She mounted the wooden walkway and went up the street.

Hey, he called.

She kept on. He stood in the street with his mouth working dryly and the purse in his hand with the money peeking out.

Yes, the man said. They is one stocks here. Name of Deitch. Is that the one you was a-huntin?

I never did know his name, she said.

Well what did he look like?

I ain't able to say that neither, she said. I never knowed they was all different kinds.

The man leaned slightly over the counter and focused his

eyes for a moment somewhere about her middle. She lowered her arms and looked away toward the sunbright windows at the front of the store.

What was it you wanted with him? the man said.

He's got somethin belongs to me I got to get from him.

And what is that?

I cain't tell ye.

You don't know that either.

I mean I know it but I cain't tell it.

Well I just thought maybe he could leave it here for ye.

Well, she said, it wouldn't keep. Sides I don't know as that is the feller. He ain't got no little chap with him is he?

I don't know, the man said. But I don't see how you goin to find him and you not knowin his name nor nothin.

I reckon I'll just have to hunt him, she said.

Well, I hope ye luck.

I thank ye.

Yes. Listen, maybe you could leave word if you wanted, write it down and I'd give it to him if it was a secret and then if it was him he'd know and could . . .

He don't know me neither, she said.

He don't.

No sir.

Well.

It's all right. I never meant to put ye out none. And I do thank ye for your trouble.

Yes, the man said. He watched her go, his jaw slightly ajar. Before she reached the door he called to her. She turned, mantled by the noon light that came crooked through the bleary panes of glass.

Yes, she said.

Do you want me to tell him that you're huntin him? Or that they is somebody huntin him? Or that . . .

No, she said. I'd take it as a favor if you'd not say nothin to him a-tall.

The cowbell clanked over the door, and again, faint and dimly pastoral in the iron gloom of the shop. He shook his head in great doubt.

When she approached they were all sitting in the wagon eating.

Howdy, the man said. Did ye get your errands run?

Yessir, she said.

Did ye find him?

No sir. He never came thisaway I don't believe. I ast.

Well.

I was just wonderin could I maybe ride back with ye'ns this evenin.

I would say ye could.

I'd be much obliged.

The old woman had risen and was staring down at her as if beset by dogs or some worse evil. The two girls were whispering and peering from behind their hands.

Set down, mamma, the woman said.

Set her out some dinner, the man said.

Lord, she said, I just ain't a bit hungry.

The woman had taken up the pail and now she stopped, still chewing, looking down at the young woman standing in the road.

Set her out some dinner, he said again.

While she ate she saw the boy coming across the mall toward them. When he saw her sitting on the edge of the wagon bed he stopped and then came on more slowly, limping.

Where you been? the woman said.

I'd as soon not hear, said the old crone.

I ain't been nowheres.

You about missed dinner.

Shoot, he said.

It was late afternoon when they set forth again, out from the town, the wheels rasping in the sand, back down the yellow road. Night fell upon them dark and starblown and the wagon grew swollen near mute with dew. On their chairs in such black immobility these travelers could have been stone figures quarried from the architecture of an older time.

HE HAD BEEN LISTENING to his own feet in the road for a long time now when the man spoke. The man said: What do ye say buddy.

Howdy, Holme said, stopping.

The man was leaning against a small walnut tree, his feet sprawled in the grass before him, one eye squinted in a kind of baleful good humor and a piece of dockweed sprouting from the corner of his mouth. He spared a wincing smile to this traveler. Set a spell and rest, he said, removing the weed and pointing at the ground with it.

I guess I better not.

Just for a minute and I'll go up the road with ye.

Well.

Sure.

He came slowly through the dusty grass, toward the shade and sat a little way from the man.

Hot ain't it?

He allowed that it was. The man bore a faint reek of

whiskey. He did not look at Holme but stared out at the road, smiling a little to himself.

Where ye goin? he said.

Just up the road.

That right? That's where I'm a-goin. Just up the road. He tapped absently at his knee with the weed, smiling. Just up the road, he said again. He turned his head as if to see were anyone looking, then reached beneath his coat where it lay on the ground alongside him and brought forth a bottle blown from purple glass, holding it up in his two hands and shaking it. He looked at Holme. Care for a little drink?

Might take just a sup.

The man handed him the bottle. Get ye a good drink, he said.

Holme twisted loose the stopper and held the bottle to his nose for a moment and then drank. His eyes shifted focus and he sat very erect. He wiped his mouth and plugged the bottle and handed it back.

I thank ye, he said.

Good ain't it?

It is.

You welcome.

He scooped the sweat from his forehead with one finger. The man sat watching the road, the weedstem twirling in his mouth and the threadthin shadow of it going long and short upon his face like a sundial's hand beneath a sun berserk. After a moment he turned to Holme again. How will ye trade boots? he said.

Holme recoiled. He looked at the boots and he looked at

the boots the man wore. I don't believe we could work up no trade hardly, he said. I just come by these.

They look to be stout'ns, the man said. What did ye have to give for em?

I don't know. I traded work for em.

I guess a man'd have to put in a few days to come by such boots as them, wouldn't he?

A few.

The man smiled again. These old shoes of mine is about give out, he said.

Holme looked at him but he had fallen to watching the road again with a kind of dreamy indolence.

You live hereabouts? Holme said.

The man's eyes swung on him. I live over at Walker's Mill, he said. Other side of Cheatham. And I'd best be getting there. He took the weed from his mouth and spat. You ready? he said.

Holme stood. The man reached and got his coat and put the bottle in one pocket. He swung it loosely over his shoulder and rose and Holme followed him into the road where the afternoon sun fell upon them brightly. Holme watched the dust bloom from under the man's bootsoles. The leather was dried and broken and the backseam of one was split and mended with bailing wire at the top. When he stepped the gash opened and closed rhythmically and his calf winked from the rent in time to the dull thump of the bottle against his back.

How far is it to where you're goin? Holme said.

Three or four mile. Tain't far.

What brings you up thisaway?

I come over to hive a swarm of bees for a man.

Holme nodded. I guess you traded it out in that there whiskey, he said.

I won that whiskey on a bet, the man said. Hivin em with no beeface and no smoker.

You get stung?

I ain't never been stung, the man said.

I reckon you've worked a good bit with bees.

Some, he said. He swung the coat in a capelike arc about him and hung it over the other shoulder. Some, he said again. He pursed his lips and blew, as if wearied. How far is it to where you're goin?

I don't know, Holme said. Just to this here town I reckon.

The beehiver looked at him sideways and away again. Or do ye not know where it is you're a-goin?

I don't know, Holme said.

Why are ye goin then?

Goin where?

The beehiver didn't answer. After a while he said: Well, say to that clump of sumac yander, pointing minutely with one finger from the hand that held his coat.

I'm lookin for my sister, Holme said.

That right? Where's she at?

Holme watched the dry sand welt under his new boots. If I knowed, he said, I'd not have to look.

The beehiver ignored this. He was looking about him. They passed the sumacs and he said: I don't see her.

Holme looked at him dully. After a while the man swung

down his coat again and this time he brought forth the bottle. Drink? he said.

All right.

He handed the bottle across without looking. Holme took it and paused in the middle of the road with his feet spread, watching above the cone of bright glass receding from his face the slow wheel of a hawk. The man watched him. When he was done he held out the bottle and the man drank and stowed it again in his pocket and they went on.

How far you come? the man said.

Pretty good piece. I don't know . . . I was over in Johnson County some.

Never been thew Cheatham though?

Not to recollect it I ain't.

You would recollect it.

Is that right?

That is right. He kicked with his toe the flat dried shell of a wheelcrushed toad. They got the awfullest jail in the state.

I ain't never been in jail, Holme said.

You ain't never been in Cheatham.

Holme put his hands in the bib of his overalls.

What trade do ye follow? the man said.

I ain't got nary.

The man nodded.

I can work, Holme said. I ain't no slack hand.

You aim to hunt work in Cheatham?

I'd studied it.

He nodded again. They went on. They forded a small branch and the beehiver bent and scooped a palmful of water at his face and whoofed and shook his head. He ran one hand through his hair and then down the side of his breeches to dry it.

How much further is it? Holme said.

Tain't far.

You reckon this here water is fit to drink?

It's old swampwater, he said.

I'm kindly takin a thirst.

The beehiver smiled his little smile and slung the coat upon his shoulder again and they went on.

They entered the town in the early afternoon. A small town of clustered frame buildings that sat plumbless and unpainted in the glary heat and listed threatfully. There did not appear to be anyone about.

They ain't much of anybody around, is they? Holme said.

Not much.

Whichaway do you go?

I go straight on thew.

They walked down the shaded side of the square and the upper windows watched them with wrinkled sun-stricken glass.

You don't know where I might ast about work do ye? Holme said.

The beehiver nodded toward the buildings along which they passed. You might try the store. See if anybody knows. Other'n that I cain't help ye.

All right, Holme said. Thank ye.

I don't think you'll thank me.

Holme had stopped but the man did not turn. Nor look, nor gesture a farewell. He diminished down the road and out of the square, swung the coat once again to his other shoulder and was gone.

Holme went on up the walkway loudly in his boots until he came to the Cheatham Mercantile. He peered through the window into the dust and gloom but he couldn't see anyone about. When he tried the door it opened and he entered cautiously. A clerk sprang up from the counter where he had been sleeping. Howdy, Holme said.

Yessir, said the clerk.

I wonder could I get a drink of water from ye.

Yessir. Right yonder in the box.

Thank ye, Holme said. He got the waterjug and drank until he could no longer breathe. He stood panting for a moment and then drank again.

Gets thirsty on a hot day don't it? the clerk said.

Holme nodded. He put the lid on the jar and set it back in the cooler. Where's everbody at? he said.

Lord I don't know. Some kind of commotion over twards the church. They left out of here like a bunch of chickens. Had to go see whatever it was.

They did?

Ever able soul of em.

Holme ran his hands along the seam of his overalls and fingered the wrapped coins in his bib. They any work hereabouts? he said.

You huntin a job?

I could use one.

Lord I wisht I could let ye have this'n. I'm about ready to thow it over.

Well I ain't much at figures. I'm lookin more for just a workin job.

Well, I don't know, the clerk said. You could ast. His eyes were wandering about dementedly.

When do ye reckon anybody'll be back.

Shhh, cautioned the clerk. He took a wire flyswat from the counter and poised stealthily. Holme watched. The clerk swung and flattened a huge melonstriped fly against a cracker-jar.

When do ye reckon they'll be anybody back, Holme said.

Any time. They been over there half the mornin.

You say they at the church?

Yep. First time in a long time for more than a few in that bunch.

Where's it at?

The church? Just right up here, the clerk pointing. Where the old'n was at fore it burnt.

Holme nodded vaguely, leaning against the drinkbox.

Where was it you said you was from?

I come up from Johnson County.

I ain't never been down there, the clerk said.

No.

That's supposed to be a mean place.

Well, I don't know. Some, I reckon.

That's what they say. I ain't never been down there.

Holme nodded. Shadows washed across the yellow light in

the storewindows, spilled through over the merchandise. Boot-treads clattered on the board porch.

Here come some now, the clerk said.

Holme went to the door and looked out. There were people milling about. Men were coming into the square on foot and aback mules and horses. Some bore arms. Behind them came a long fieldwagon drawn by two white mules and attended by small boys. Heralding this spectacle there came like the last rank bloom of battlesmoke a pall of near white dust drifting over the square.

What is it? the clerk said.

I cain't tell, Holme said. Some kind of a big to-do.

Ast them fellers on the porch yonder.

Holme leaned from the door and several of the men looked at him. What is it? he said.

They just now bringin em in, one said.

Who?

Them, the man said.

Another one looked past him at Holme. Them bodies, he said.

A young boy turned and looked up at them. Them old dead people, he said.

Holme watched with them while the wagon rumbled down the square. He could feel the clerk's breath cold on his sweat-soaked back.

Who is it? he said.

I don't know, Holme said. They ain't told.

How many was they kilt?

He never said. Several I reckon.

The wagon passed slowly before them in its wake of pale dust, the mules clean and elegant and the driver upon the box somber and erect. On the bed of the wagon behind him in a row were three wooden coffins. They were fluted and wormbored and hung with webbed clots of yellow clay. Each had been ripped open at the top and from one of them trailed in stained pennants some rags of leached and tattered and absolutely colorless satin.

Lord God, the clerk whispered.

The wagon passed. The driver raised his hands almost imperceptibly, the reins quivered along the mules' flanks and they came to rest. The men on the porch turned to watch. Holme could see the driver stand out of the wagon above their heads and then descend and he could see the ears of one mule dip and twitch. He turned to the clerk. Them old boxes has been in the ground, he said.

I see they has.

What all do you reckon . . .

I believe somebody has dug em up. Punch that feller there. Hey Bill.

They spoke in hoarse whispers. The man leaned one ear toward them.

Listen, what all's happent? said the clerk.

I don't know. Somebody has dug up a bunch of graves at the church.

Grave thiefs, another whispered.

They Lord have mercy.

Yonder comes the high sheriff now.

Two men were coming across the square on horses, talking to each other. The crowd fanned before them and they dismounted and tied at the rail and went into a building there.

There were now several hundred people clustered about the wagon and they began to talk in a rising babble of voices. The sun stood directly over them. It seemed hung there in glaring immobility, as if perhaps arrested with surprise to see above the earth again these odds of morkin once commended there. The men along the walk had begun to file past, some standing on toe tips, to view the remains in the wagon bed.

I don't believe I care to look, the clerk said.

Holme found himself moving down the walk with the crowd. Above the odor of sweat and manure he could smell the musty decay of the boxes. When he came abreast of the wagon he could see a waxen gray face scowling eyelessly at the bright noon. In the next box lay what appeared to have been an old man. The box was lined with cheap quilted satin, the figure within wore a white shirt and a necktie but no coat or trousers. The flesh on those old legs had drawn and withered and gone a dusty brown. Someone should have cared more than to leave an old man halfnaked in his burial box beneath these eyes and such a sun. But that was not all. Across the desiccated chest lay a black arm, and when Holme stood on his toes he could see that the old man shared his resting place with a negro sexton whose head had been cut half off and who clasped him in an embrace of lazarous depravity.

Holme shuffled past. The man in front of him turned. Ain't that a sight, he said. Holme nodded.

I reckon whoever done it will be wearin a black suit.

Holme looked at the man who spoke.

I hate knowin they is such people, don't you?

He nodded again. They were moving back up the street toward the store. The clerk was talking to a number of men on the porch. When he saw Holme he cut his eyes away quickly. He went on talking. One of the men turned and looked at Holme. Holme stood in the square idly. After a few minutes two more turned and looked at him. He began to shift about uneasily. A man came away from the group and started down the walk toward the wagon, pushing his way past the crowd there. Just before he entered the building where the sheriff had gone he turned again and looked in Holme's direction. Holme started across the square, walking slowly. He was listening behind him very hard. When he reached the corner he looked back. Three men were crossing the square at a fast walk. He began to run. He ran down a narrow lane, looking for a turn. He could not hear them behind him. He passed a long wooden shed and at the end of it was an alleyway beyond which he could see a field and cattle. He took this turn and checked behind him once again. They came leisurely and with grim confidence. He went into the alley and along the rear of the shed. Two negroes were unloading sacks of feed from a wagon at a dock. They watched him pass. He came to a stile at the fence and vaulted through it and out into the field, quartering slightly to the left toward a line of trees. A group of cows raised their muzzles out of the grass and regarded him with bland placidity. He raced through a perpetual explosion of insects and his breath was already coming hard for him. When he reached the line of trees there was a fence again and he stumbled over it. They were coming across the field at what looked to be a trot. Behind them came more. Their voices floated in the droning emptiness. He ducked into the shelter of the woods, turned down a stone gully washed bare of leaves, running.

When he came out on the creek a colony of small boys erupted from a limestone ledge like basking seals alarmed and pitched white and naked into the water. They watched him with wide eyes, heads bobbing. He crossed at the shallows above them with undiminished speed, enclosed in a huge fan of water, and plunged into a canebrake on the far side. Crakes, plovers, small birds clattered up out of the dusty bracken into the heat of the day and cane rats fled away before him with thin squeals. He crashed on blindly. When he emerged from the brake he was in a road, appearing suddenly in a final and violent collapse of stalks like someone fallen through a prop inadvertently onstage, looking about in terror of the open land that lay there and still batting at the empty caneless air before him for just a moment before turning and lurching back into the brake. He went on at a trot, one eye walled to the sun for a sextant and his heart pumping in his gorge. When he came out of the cane again he was in deep woods. He paused to get his breath and listen but he could hear nothing save his pounding blood. Then he was kneeling like something broken or penitent among the corrugate columns. A dove called softly and ceased. He was kneeling in wild iris and mayapple, his palms spread on his thighs. He raised his head and looked at the high sun and the light falling long and plumb through the forest. No sounds of chase or distant cries reached him in this green serenity. He rose to his feet and went on. Nightfall found him crouched in a thicket, waiting. With full dark he came forth, a solitary traveler going south. He walked all night. Not even a dog spoke him down that barren road.

When he talked to the man with the barn roof he had eaten nothing but some early field turnips for two days. He had washed and shaved in a branch and tried to wash the shirt. The collar of it was frayed open and the white cheesecloth lining stood about his neck with a kind of genteel shabbiness like a dickie of ruined lace.

You paint? the man said.

Sure, he said. I paint all the time.

The man looked him over. I got a barn roof needs paintin, he said. You do roofs?

I done lots of roofs, he said.

You contract or just do day wages?

Holme wiped his lips with two fingers. Well, he said, if it ain't but just the one roof I'd as soon do wages.

You pretty fast on roofs?

I make right good time on a roof.

The man regarded him a moment more. All right, he said. I pay a dollar a day. You want to start tomorrow I'll get the paint this evenin and have it ready for ye.

That suits me, he said. What time you want me to start?

We start here at six. Ceptin the nigger. He gets down early on account of the feedin.

Holme nodded.

All right, the man said.

He started away.

Where you stayin at? the man said.

Holme stopped. Well, I've not found a place as yet. I just got here.

You can stay in the barn if ye ain't proud, the man said. You goin to be on it all day you might as well get under it at night.

All right, Holme said. I thank ye.

I don't want no smokin in there.

I ain't never took it up, Holme said.

From the roof ridge he could see a good distance over the rolling country. He adjusted his ladders and sat for a moment, watching the sun bleed across the east, watching a small goat go along the road. The rusted weathercock cried soft above him in the morning wind. He kneaded the bristles of his brush and adjusted his bucket. His shadow moiled cant and baneful over the lot below him and over the waking land a chorale of screaming cocks waned and ceased and began again. When the sun struck the eastern bank of the roof the water drew steaming up the tin and vanished almost instantly. He stirred the thick green paste and began.

By midmorning the roof had reached such a temperature that the wet paint flashed on the tin like lacquer. The paint in the bucket healed over when he rested, and the base of the brush had taken on a skirt of dull green scum. He continued along, marking his progress by the crimped panels. Through the haze of heat rising from the roof he watched a girl come and go from the house with washing, watched her move along the line in the yard, stooping at her basket and reaching up, and the shape of her breasts pulling against the cloth. Paint seeped from the uplifted handle down his poised wrist. He scraped it away with one finger and slapped the paint out of the butt of the brush. He watched her go in again.

By afternoon of the third day he had done one half of the roof and had moved his ladder to the other side, the ladder hanging from the ridge by its cleats, the bucket balanced in the rungs and him painting his way down the first panel. If they had come the day before or even that morning he would not have seen them. They were four, already in the barnlot and coming down the fence high-footed in the green bog of manure and mud. One had a shotgun and the others carried slats, their faces upturned brightly, watching him. He set the brush down, wedging it under a rung, and started up the ladder toward the top, coming erect on the peak and walking it carefully, watching his boots, until he was above the ground ladder. He squatted on his heels and coasted to it, braking with his hands and the soles of his boots and then almost overriding it. He heard one of them yell. He looked down again to see them but they had come under the lee of the barn.

Head him, one of them called.

Other side, Will, other side.

Run him around thisaway and I'll break him down like a shotgun.

He came down the ladder frontways, half running, falling

the last six feet and stumbling up again, running along the side of the barn. At the corner a man sprang up, a face pale and contorted in a whitelipped smile, and brought the slat flatwise across his back with a sound that exploded clear through him. He went headlong in the dried chaff, not even stopping, running again from the ground up and across the fence through the hoglot where a boar came up out of a wallow with a scream and charged him and across the far fence and into the upper pasture. He could hear the man behind him saying Goddamn, Goddamn, leaping and stepping as the boar came at him, trying to get back to the fence and saying You son of a bitch you, and the boar screaming and cutting at him and him sliding and dancing in the mud and above it all the whack of the slat on the boar's hide.

He went on, through waisthigh grass, listening for the shot until his head hummed. It didn't come. When he topped out on the hill he turned to look back. They were deployed across the field a hundred yards below him. They stopped, one and the next and the third and the last as if wired together and the one with the shotgun raised it and a black flower bloomed about him. Holme wheeled. The pellets went up his back like wasps. He winced and put one hand to his neck and came away with a thin smear of blood and already he was running again. He came down out of the field running and into a pine wood at the bottom running hard on the open ground with the trees dodging past. When he fell he slid his length again headlong in the pineneedles, rising out of a dark trough with swatches of them stuck to the paint and blood on his palms. When he looked back he had seized his wild face in both hands as if main strength were needed to look there and when he went on he went at a crazed pace deeper into the woods.

He came out upon a ravine and ran along it until it began to draw away to the right and then he plunged and slid down the embankment and leaped to clear the creek at the bottom. But the soft turf gave beneath his foot and he went face down in the water. When he tried to rise he could not. He got himself propped on his elbows, gasping, listening. The creek murmured away down the dark ravine. He leaned his face into the shallow water and drank, choking, and after a while he vomited. And after a while he drank again.

He wore a shapeless and dusty suit of black linen that was small on him and his beard and hair were long and black and tangled. He wore neither shirt nor collar and his bare feet were out at the toes of a pair of handmade brogans. He said nothing. They gave before him until he reached the wagon and stood looking down at the man in the bed of it. They waited, a mass of grave faces. He turned slowly and looked about him. It's old man Salter, one said. Dead. Stabbed and murdered. He nodded. All right, he said. Let's be for findin the man that done it. And in the glare of the torches nothing of his face visible but the eyes like black agates, nothing of his beard or the suit he wore gloss enough to catch the light and nothing about his hulking dusty figure other than its size to offer why these townsmen should follow him along the road this night.

In the cool and smoking dawn there hung from a blackhaw tree in a field on the edge of the village the bodies of two itinerant millhands. They spun slowly in turn from left to right and back again. As if charged with some watch. That and the slight flutter of their hair in the morning wind was all the movement there was about them.

ONCE IN THE NIGHT she heard a horse coming along over the country road, a burning horse beneath the dead moonlight that trailed a wake of pale and drifting dust. She could hear the labored breath and harness creak and the clink of its iron caparisons and then the hoofs exploded over the planking of the bridge. Dust and fine gravel sifted down upon her and hissed in the water. The pounding faded down the road to the faintest sound of heartbeat and the heartbeat was in her own thin chest. She pulled the stained bundle of clothing closer beneath her face and slept again.

She slept through the first wan auguries of dawn, gently washed with river fog while martins came and went among the arches. Slept into the first heat of the day and woke to see toy birds with sesame eyes regarding her from their clay nests overhead. She rose and went to the river and washed her face and dried it with her hair. When she had gathered up the bundle of her belongings she emerged from beneath the bridge and set forth along the road again. Emaciate and blinking and with the wind among her rags she looked like something replevied by grim miracle from the ground and sent with tattered windings and halt corporeality into the agony of sunlight. Butterflies attended her and birds dusting in the road did not fly up when she passed. She hummed to herself as she went some child's song from an old dead time.

In half a mile she began to come upon houses and barns, fields in which crude implements lay idled. She went more slowly. She could smell food cooking. The house she chose was a painted frame house that stood in a well-tended yard. She approached, wary of dogs, up a walkway past rank growths of beebalm and phlox terraced with fieldstone, past latticed morning glories strung against the blinding white clapboards. Bonneted and bent to the black earth a woman with a trowel, a small cairn of stones and a paper of plants beside her.

Howdy, she said.

The woman looked over her shoulder, sat back on her heels and tapped the clods from the trowel. Mornin, she said. Can I help you?

Yes mam. I'm huntin the lady of the house.

Well, you found her.

Yes mam. What I was wonderin was if maybe you needed some house help or not.

The woman rose, dusting her skirts with the backs of her hands. Her eyes were very blue even in the shade of her bonnet. Help, she said. Yes. I reckon it looks like I need a gardener, don't it?

It's a right pretty garden. As pretty a one as I've seed.

Well thank you.

Yes mam.

You married?

No mam.

In other words you could stay on.

Yes mam.

Regular?

Well, I don't know right off for how long. You ain't said if you needed me.

I don't need somebody for just a week. I had them kind. More trouble than they're worth. Who was it told you I needed a girl?

Nobody.

Nobody sent you?

No mam. I just come by myself. To ast if maybe you did.

You're not one of them Creech girls are you?

No mam. I'm a Holme.

The woman smiled and she smiled back. The woman said: That's my granddaughter now. Then she heard it, a child's wail from within the house.

They're here the rest of this week. You come along while I see about her.

She followed the woman along the stone path to the rear of the house where they entered through the kitchen, the woman taking down her bonnet and laying it across a chair, saying: Just sit down and rest a minute and I won't be long.

She sat. Already she could feel it begin warm and damp, sitting there holding her swollen breasts, feeling it in runnels down her belly until she pressed the cloth of her dress against it, looking down at the dark stains.

Mam.

Yes? The woman turning at the door.

About workin here . . . I don't believe . . .

Yes, just a minute now, I won't be a minute.

She heard the woman on the steps, treading upward into the sound of the child's crying until both ceased, and she rose and left for them the empty room with table and stove and cooking pots, holding her own things to her breast where thin blue milk welled from the rotting cloth, going down the path to the road again.

She went on through the town past houses and yard gardens with tomatoes and beans yellowed with road dust and poles rising skewed into the hot air, past rows of new corn putting up handhigh through the gray loam, along old fences of wormy rail, the spurs of dust from her naked heels drifting arcwise in pale feathers to the road again. If crows had not risen from a field she might never have looked that way to see two hanged men in a tree like gross chimes.

She stood for a moment watching them, clutching the bundle of clothes, wondering at such dark work in the noon of day while all about sang summer birds. She went on, walking softly. Once she looked back. Nothing moved in that bleak tree.

Further along she spied a planting of turnips. She crossed a fence and made her way toward them over the turned black earth. They were already seeding and she could smell the musty hemlock odor of them sweet in the air. They were small, bitter, slightly soft. She pulled half a dozen and cleaned away the dirt with the gathered hem of her dress. While she was chewing the first of them a voice hallooed across the field. She could see a house and a barn beyond the curve in the road and now in the barnlot she made out a man there watching her. His voice drifted over the hot spaces lost and thin:

Get out of them turnips.

She looked at the handful of turnips, at him, then broke off the tops of them and pushed the bulbs into her parcel and started back to the road. When she reached the house the man was standing there waiting for her. She swallowed and nodded to him. Mornin, she said.

Mornin eh? You've had a long day of it. What are you doin roguin in my garden?

I wouldn't of took nothin if I'd knowed anybody cared. It was just some little old thin turnips. I've not eat today.

Ain't? How come you ain't? You ain't run off from somewheres are ye?

No, she said. I ain't even got nowheres to run off from.

He considered this for a moment, one eye almost shut. If you ain't got nowheres to run from you must not have no place to run to. Where is it you are goin if it's any of my business?

I'm startin to wish it was somebody else's besides just mine.

I believe you've run off from somewheres, the man said.

I've been run off from.

Ah, said the man. He looked her up and down.

I'm a-huntin this here tinker, she said.

Tinker?

Yessir. He's got somethin belongs to me.

I'll bet he does.

I got to get it back.

And what is it?

I cain't tell ye. He knows he ain't supposed to have it. If I can just see him.

That sounds more than just commonly curious to me, the man said. Where's your family at?

I ain't got nary'n. Ceptin just a brother and he run off. So I got to find this here tinker.

The man shook his head. You ain't goin to get no satisfaction out of no tinker. Specially if you ain't got no kin to back ye up. I'm surprised myself you ain't got no more shame than to tell that it was one.

They Lord, she said, it ain't nothin like that. I ain't never even seen him.

You ort to of knowed one'd do ye dirt . . . You what?

I ain't never seen him.

You ain't.

No sir.

The man stood watching her for a moment. Honey, he said, I think you better get in out of the sun.

I wouldn't care to myself, she said.

Go on to the house and tell my old woman I said you was to take dinner with us. Go on now. I'll be in directly I get unhitched and watered.

Well, she said, you sure it's all right. I don't want to put nobody out.

Go on, he said. I'll be in directly, tell her.

He watched her go, shaking his head slowly. She crossed the scored and grassless yard warding away chickens with a little shooing gesture until she arrived at the door and tapped.

The woman who appeared had a buttermold in one hand and in the other a gathering of apron with which she wiped her face. The sight of this frail creature upon her stoop seemed to weary her. What is it? she said.

Your man said was it all right I was to come for . . . He said to ast you if you'd not care to let me take dinner with ye'ns if . . .

She didn't appear to be listening. She was looking at this petitioner with a kind of aberrant austerity. I've churned till I'm plumb give out, she said.

It is a chore, ain't it.

Plumb give out. She held the buttermold before her now in her two hands, sacrificially.

Yes mam. Your man yander sent me. He said to tell you he'd be along in just a minute.

She looked the young woman up and down. It's half a hour till dinner, she said. You would expect somebody to know what time dinner was after nineteen year now wouldn't ye?

Yes mam, she said, looking down.

It's when I ring it, that's when it is.

I didn't know, she said.

Him, not you. Where's he at?

He went to water.

Did he? She clapped the mold absently. Funny the way a man's day gets shorter and a woman's longer. And you're here for dinner are ye?

If it ain't no trouble.

Trouble? No trouble. Since I got a maid and a cook now it ain't. Come in

She went past and into the kitchen.

Get ye a chair. I'm just cleanin up this mess.

I'd be proud to help.

Just set. I'll be done directly.

All right.

Not there. It's broke.

All right.

She watched while the older woman ladled the last of the butter from the bottom of the churn into the mold and pressed it out.

That's a sight of butter.

The woman was clearing away the things. She glanced at the hives of butter aligned on a board down the table. It ain't near what I do in the winter, she said. They's two different stores carries my butter.

The other folded her hands over the stained bundle of rags in her lap. I reckon that would keep a body busy with churnin.

It'd keep one busy just milkin. She ran the wooden blade of her ladle down the dasher.

Is it just you and your man here?

It is. We raised five. All dead.

She had been going to nod interest or approval but now

her jaw fell and her hands knotted in her lap. In the silence of the kitchen only the dull sound of wood on buttered wood.

You'd think a man's hand would fit a cow's tit wouldn't ye? the woman said.

She looked down at her feet and placed them very carefully together. I don't know, she said.

You ain't married?

No mam.

Well. You ever get married I expect you'll find out they don't.

Yes mam. Can I not help ye with nothin sure enough?

Near done now. Don't need no help. You just set.

All right.

Four girls.

She sat, hands folded. The woman dampened cheesecloth to lay over the butter.

Oldest'n been near your age I reckon.

I'm nineteen, she said.

Yes. Oldest'n be just about your age. He ain't comin is he?

She raised her head slightly and looked out the one small window. No mam. Not that I can see.

All right.

It's faired off to be a right nice day ain't it?

Yes. I don't even know whether you'd say raised or not when they wasn't but just young. The boy was near a growed man when he died.

Yes mam. I'm sorry you've had such troubles.

Mm-hmm. Sorry. Don't need sorry. Not in this house. Sorry laid the hearth here. Sorry ways and sorry people and heavensent grief and heartache to make you pine for your death.

She was watching her toes.

For nineteen year.

Yes mam.

I believe that's him now, she said. Called or not. You can look and see if that ain't him now if you will.

It's him, she said.

All right. We'll eat directly he gets washed. If he's washin.

When the man entered the house he nodded to her and went on through the door to the next room without speaking to the woman. She could hear him puttering about at some task. The woman raised aloft a stove-eye in black and steaming consecration and poked the fire. A gout of pale smoke ascended and flattened itself against the ceiling. It was very quiet in the kitchen. Flies droned back and forth. When the man came in again he skirted the table and sat at the far end and folded his hands before him on the oilcloth.

Hidy, she said.

Howdy. I expect you could use a bite to eat by now.

I ast could I help but she said she'd rather to do it her own self.

She does everthing by herself.

The woman opened the oven door and slid forth a tray of cornbread.

That's finelookin butter ain't it? That she's made.

I cain't eat it, the man said.

Her joined hands went to her lips for a moment and returned to her lap again.

Cain't eat it. Makes me sicker'n a dog.

I guess they's some things everbody cain't . . . I guess everbody has got somethin he cain't eat.

What's yourn?

What?

I said what's yourn? That you cain't eat. It ain't turnips I don't reckon.

She was watching her hands, yellow skin tautening over the knuckles. I don't know, she said.

No.

A body gets hungry I reckon will eat pret-near anything.

I've heard that. I'm proud I ain't never gone hungry.

It's best not to have to. I reckon.

It's best not to have to do lots of things. Like hunt somebody you never heard of . . . Was that not it?

Never seen, she said.

Never seen then. And I reckon sleep wherever dark fell on ye. Or worse.

The woman lifted her head to toss back the hair from her face. Leave her alone, she said. She ain't botherin you.

Just get it on the table, woman. You don't need to be concerned about nothin else.

Don't you pay him no mind. He's meanhearted and sorry and they ain't nothin to be done for him.

That's all right, she said. We was just talkin.

The man's speckled hands had drawn up clenched like two great dying spiders on either side of the empty white plate that sat before him. You flaptongued old bat, don't call me sorry. I'll show you what sorry is if you want.

The woman flung her head above the stove again. O yes, she said. That's nice for company now ain't it?

Goddamn you and some company both, the man said, rising. Don't come on with that fancy shit to me about some company. If you looked to your own a little better and companied less . . .

What? she said, turning. What? You've got the nerve to thow my family up to me?

Your family? Why damn you and your family to everlasting shit. You know what I'm talkin about . . .

She had risen from the table with her parcel beneath one arm and moved to the nearest wall, watching this tableau with widening eyes. The spoon made a vicious slicing sound, crossing the room in a wheel of sprayed stew. The man scooped up one of the bricks of butter and let fly with it. It hung in a yellow blob on the warmer door for a moment before it dropped with a hiss to the top of the stove.

You leave my butter alone, the woman said. Don't you lay a hand on that butter.

She eased her way along the wall to the door and got the handle under her fingers, turned it, backing carefully out as it opened. She saw the man smile. The last thing she saw before she turned and ran was the board of butter aloft, the woman screaming. As she crossed the yard the breakage mounted crash on crash into a final crescendo of shattered glass and then silence in which she could hear stricken sobs. She did not look back. When she reached the road she slowed to a fast walk and soon she was limping along with one hand to her side and bent against the stitch of pain there. When she had put two bends in the road between her and the house she stopped to rest in the grass at the roadside until the pain was gone. She was very hungry. She wanted to wait for the chance of a wagon coming but after she had waited a long time and no wagon came she went on again.

She passed the last of the cleared land and the road went down into a deep and marshy wood. Cattails and arrowheads grew in the ditches and in the stands of pollenstained water where sunning turtles tilted from stones and logs at her approach. She went this way for miles. It was late afternoon before she came to any house at all and it a slattern shack all but hidden among the trees.

And she could not have said to what sex belonged the stooped and hooded anthropoid that came muttering down the fence toward her. In one hand a hoe handled crudely with a sapling stave, an aged face and erupting from beneath some kind of hat lank hair all hung with clots like a sheep's scut, stumbling along in huge brogans and overalls. She stopped at the sight of this apparition. The road went in deep woods and constant damp and the house was grown with a rich velour of moss and lichen and brooded in a palpable miasma of rot. Chickens had so scratched the soil from the yard that knobs and knees of treeroots stood everywhere in grotesque configuration up out of the earth like some gathering of the mad laid suddenly bare in all their writhen attitudes of pain. She waited. It was an old woman spoke to her:

I've not been a-hoein. This here is just to kill snakes with.

She nodded.

I don't ast nobody's sayso for what all I do but I'd not have ye to think I'd been a-hoein.

Yes, she said.

I don't hold with breakin the sabbath and don't care to associate with them that does.

It ain't sunday, she said.

It's what?

It ain't sunday today, she said.

The old woman peered at her strangely. I don't believe you been saved have ye? she said.

I don't know.

Ah, the old woman said, one of them. She tamped down a small piece of earth with the flat of the hoe.

You live here, I reckon.

The old woman looked up. I have lived here nigh on to forty-seven year. Since I was married.

It's a nice cool place here, she said.

O yes. This is a shady spot here. I don't allow no wood cut near the house.

She could see that the porch of the house was ricked end to end with cords of stovewood and the one window which faced them held back in webbed and dusty tiers more wood yet. Is it just you and the mister at home now? she said.

Earl died, she said.

Oh.

I just despise a snake don't you?

Yes mam.

I'm like my granny that way. She always said what she despised worst in the world was snakes hounds and sorry women.

Yes mam.

I won't have a hound on the place.

No mam.

The old woman drew up the wings of her nose between her thumb and forefinger and sneezed forth a spray of mucus and wiped her fingers on the overalls she wore.

Earl's daddy used to keep half a holler full of old beat-up hounds. He had to keep Earl's too. I won't have one on the place. Wantin to lay out half the night runnin in the woods with a bunch of dogs like somethin crazy. Ain't a bit of use in the world somebody puttin up with such as that. I run his daddy off too. Told him he'd run with hounds so hard and long he'd took on the look of one let alone the smell. And him a squire. They wasn't no common people but I declare if they didn't have some common habits among em. He's a squire ye know. Course that never kept his daughter from runnin off with a no-account that sent her back big in the belly and thin in the shanks and nary word from him ever from that day to this. Or doomsday if ye wanted to wait. How far are ye goin?

Just up the road. I'm travelin.

Where to?

Well. I mean I'm not goin to just one place in particular.

The old woman cocked her elf's face and peered at her with eyes gone near colorless with years. The thin and ropy hands with which she clutched the handle of the hoe opened and closed. Maybe you're goin to several places in particular then, she said.

No mam. Not no special places. I'm a-huntin somebody.

Who's that?

Just somebody. This feller.

The old woman's eyes went to her belly and back again.

She straightened herself and tucked the bundle of clothes beneath one arm.

Feller, the old woman said. Where's he got to?

I wisht I knowed.

The old woman nodded. It's a goodly sizeable world to set out huntin somebody in.

That's God's truth.

I hope ye luck anyways.

I thank ye.

The old woman nodded again and tapped the ground with her hoe.

Well I guess I'd best be gettin on.

Needn't to be in no hurry. Come up to the house.

Well.

I got fresh cornbread from yesterday evenin and a pot of greens and fatmeat if you're hungry a-tall. Give ye a glass of cool buttermilk anyway.

Well. If you don't care.

Shoo. Come along.

She followed the old woman up a trench of a path toward the house, the old woman poking at the knobby roots reared out of the red earth as if testing for hostile life. When they entered the house it was into nigh total dark, past ricks of wood stacked to the low ceiling and little more than a cat's passage between them, down another corridor walled in by the sawn dowel ends of sticks and split logs until they came to the kitchen, likewise crammed with wood in every available space.

Get ye a chair, the woman said.

Thank ye.

She was at the stove, turning fire up out of the dead gray ashes. Are ye not married? she said.

No mam.

She added wood. She lifted the lid from a pot crusted with blackened orts and tilted it for inspection. Her voice hollow and chambered: Where's your youngern.

What?

I said where's your youngern.

I've not got nary.

The babe, the babe, the old woman crooned.

They ain't nary'n.

Hah, said the old woman. Bagged for the river trade I'd judge. Yon sow there might make ye a travelin mate that's downed her hoggets save one.

She sat very straight in the chair. Cradled among stovewood against the wall was a sleeping hog she had not seen. The old woman turned, a small bent androgyne gesturing with a black spoon, waiting.

That's a lie what you said, the girl whispered hoarsely. I never. He was took from me. A chap. I'm a-huntin him.

Your hand to God, the old woman said.

She raised her hand slightly from the table. Yes, she said.

Aye. Where's he at now?

This here tinker has got him.

Tinker.

Yes mam. He come to the house while I was confinin. We'd been there four months or more and they'd not been nary tinker a-tall come round.

Ah. And stoled him away. I always heard they was bad about it.

She stirred uneasily in her chair. No mam, she said. My brother give it to him. Or sold it one. He tried to let on like it died but I caught him in that lie and he owned up what he done.

Your brother?

Yes mam.

And where's he at?

I don't know.

You've not lawed him?

No mam.

You ort to've.

Well. He's family.

The old woman shook her head. When was it all? she said.

Just March or April. I forgot. She looked up. The old woman was looking past her, weighing the spoon in her hand.

I think most likely it was in March.

And you was a-nursin him.

No mam. I never had the chancet. I never even seen him.

The old woman looked down at her. You goin to have to find him or let him be. One or t'other.

Yes mam.

And you best grease them paps.

Yes mam, she said.

Aye, said the old woman. I got some I'll give ye. She opened the firebox door and poked and spat among the flames and clanged it shut again. The sow reared half up and regarded them with narrow pink eyes and a look of hostile cunning. The old woman looked to her pot and then brought down a pitcher of buttermilk from her cupboard and a glass. I believe everbody loves a good drink of buttermilk, she said. Don't you?

Yes mam, she said. She was watching a woodrat that had come from a pile of kindling along the wall and now paused to scratch with one tiny hindfoot.

Yander goes a old rat, she said.

I don't have no rats in my house, the old woman said simply.

The rat looked at them and went on across the woodpile and from sight.

I cain't abide varmints of no description.

She nodded. I'm like you, she said.

I'll have us some supper here directly.

Thank ye, she said, the glass of milk in her hand, wearing a clown's mouth of it. It had darkened in the room and fire showed thin and pink in the joints of the stove's iron carriage.

They's a tinker comes thew here be it ever so little often, the old woman said. Got a jenny to pull his traps and smokes stogies. Does that favor him?

I don't know. I ain't never seen him.

The old woman paused midway unscrewing a tin of snuff. She did not look up. After a minute she undid the tin and took a pinch of the tobacco between her fingers and placed it in her lower lip. Do ye dip? she said.

No mam. I've not took it up.

She nodded and put the lid back and replaced the tin in her shirt pocket. If you ain't never seen him, she said, how do you expect to know him when ye do.

Well, she said, I don't believe he had no jenny.

Most don't.

He sells them books.

What books.

Them nasty books.

Most do. I thought you said he come to the house.

He did come to it but he never come in it.

Did you want some more buttermilk?

No thank ye mam. I've a plenty.

It's a poor lot wanderin about thataway, said the old woman.

They ain't no help for it.

And if ye find him what?

I'll just tell him. I'll tell him I want my chap. She was gesturing strangely in the air with one hand. The old woman watched her. Milk ran from the dark cloth she wore, the hand subsided into her lap again like a falling bird. I'd of wanted to see it anyways, she said. Even if it had of died.

The old woman nodded and wiped the corners of her mouth each in turn with the pursed web of her thumb. Aye, she said. Reach them plates down from behind ye now.

Yes mam.

Did you come thew Well's Station?

Yes mam. This mornin. I seen two fellers hung in a tree.

That was yesterday.

No mam. It was this mornin.

I reckon they still there then. They was supposed to of killed old man Salter over there.

It sinkened me in my heart to see it.

Yes. Here. I'll get the lamp directly.

Ain't you scared by yourself?

Some. Sometimes. Ain't you?

Yes mam. I always was scared. Even when they wasn't nobody bein murdered nowheres.

HE CAME DOWN out of the kept land and into a sunless wood where the road curved dark and cool, overlaid with immense ferns, trees hung with gray moss like hag's hair, and in this green and weeping fastness birdcalls he had not heard before. He could see no tracks in the packed sand he trod and he left none. Sometime in the afternoon he came upon a cabin and upon the veranda an old bearded man seated with a cane tilted across one knee. Two hounds watched him with bleeding eyes, muzzles flat to the scoured and grassless soil in the yard. He slowed his steps and raised one hand. The old man did not move for a minute and then his hand came slowly from his lap palmoutward no higher than his chest and returned without pausing.

Howdy, he said.

Howdy, said the old man, a voice remote and soft.

I hate to bother anybody but I was wonderin could I might get a sup of water from ye.

Wouldn't turn Satan away for a drink, the old man said. Come up.

Thank ye, he said, coming through the yard, the hounds rising surly and mistrustful and moving away.

Got a well full, the man said. Just round back. Help yourself.

Thank ye, he said again, going on with a final nod, along the side of the house to the rear where an iron pump stood on the end of a pipe a foot above the well cover, as if the ground had settled and left this shank exposed. He took up the handle and cranked it and immediately the water came up clear and full and gorged the pump's tongue and cascaded into a bucket at his feet. He watched a spider move in its web across the flume inspecting from drop to drop the water beading there. He took the gourd from the bucket and rinsed and filled it and drank. The water was cold and sweet with a faint taste of iron. He drank two dipperfuls and passed the back of his hand across his mouth and looked about him. A small garden grubbed out of the loamy soil and beyond that an impenetrable wall of poison ivy. Random stands of grass, scraggly and wheatcolored. A waste of blue clay where washwater was thrown.

The back of the house was windowless. There was a door with no handle and a stovepipe that leaned from a hole hacked through the wall with an axe. There was no sign of stock, not so much as a chicken. Holme would have said maybe it was whiskey, but it wasn't whiskey.

He went back to the man on the porch. That's fine water, he said.

The old man turned and looked down at him. Yes, he said. Tis. Know how deep that well is?

No. Fifty foot?

Not even fifteen. It's actual springwater. Used to be a spring just back of here but it dried up or sunk under the ground or somethin. Sunk, I reckon. Year of the harrykin. Blowed my chimley down. Fell out in the yard and left a big hole in the side of the house. I was settin there watchin the fire and I blinked and next thing I was lookin outside. Come mornin I went to the spring and it weren't there. So I got me a well now. Don't need all that there pump but I chancet to come by it. Good water though.

Yes it is.

Seems like everthing I get around runs off in the ground somewheres and I got to go after it.

You live here by yourself?

Not exactly. I got two hounds and a ten-gauge double-barrel that keeps me company. They's lots of meanness in these parts and I ain't the least of it.

Holme looked away. The old man tilted forward in his chair and stroked his beard and squinted.

Live by yourself and you bound to talk to yourself and when ye commence that folks start it up that you're light in the head. But I reckon it's all right to talk to a dog since most folks do even if a dog don't understand and cain't answer if he did.

Yes, Holme said.

Aye, said the old man. He tilted his chair back against the side of the house once more. It was very quiet. The hounds lay like plaster dogs in a garden.

Well, I thank ye for the drink, Holme said.

Best not be in no rush, the man said.

Well, I got to be gettin on.

Whereabouts is it you're headed?

Just up the road. I'm a-huntin work.

I doubt you can make it afore nightfall.

Make what?

Preston Flats. It's about fourteen mile.

What's between here and it?

The old man gestured toward the woods. Just like you see. More of it. They's one more house. About two mile down.

Who lives there?

They don't nobody live there now. Used to be a mink-trapper lived there but he got snakebit and died. Been snakebit afore and thowed it off. This'n got him in the neck. When they found him he was kneelin down like somebody fixin to pray. Stiff as a locust post. That's about eight year ago.

They Lord, Holme said.

Well. The old man recrossed his legs. I never did like him much anyways. Poisoned two of my dogs.

How come him to do that?

I don't know. Mayhaps he never meant to. He used to poison for varmints. They said they had to break ever bone in his body to get him laid out in his box. Coroner took a sixpound maul to him.

Holme looked at him in dull wonder and the old man looked at the steaming woods beyond the road. He lifted a twist of tobacco from the bib of his overalls and paused with it in his hand while he consulted pockets for his knife.

Chew? he said.

I thank ye, Holme said. I ain't never took it up.

The old man pared away a plug and crammed it in his mouth. Do ye drink? he asked.

I've been knowed to, Holme said.

I'd offer was I able but I ain't. Ye ain't got nary little drink tucked away in your poke have ye?

I wisht I did, Holme said.

Aye, the old man said. Clostest whiskey to here is a old nigger woman on Smith Creek and it ain't good. Sides which they's genly a bunch of mean bucks lays out down there drunk. Got knives ye could lean on. Last time I was down there you couldn't of stirred em with a stick. Makes a feller nervous. He shifted the cane to the other knee and spat. Don't it you?

I expect it would.

Listen yander, he said, tilting his head.

What's that? said Holme.

Listen.

The dogs lifted their long faces and regarded one another.

Yander they go, the old man said, pointing.

They watched a high and trembling wedge of geese drift down the sky with diminishing howls.

Used to hunt them things for a livin afore it was outlawed, the old man said. That was a long time ago. Fore you was borned I reckon. You ain't no game warden are ye?

No, Holme said.

Didn't figure ye was. You ever see a four-gauge shotgun?

No. Not to recollect it I ain't.

The old man rose from his chair. Come in till I show ye one, he said.

He led the way into the house, a two-room board shack sparsely furnished with miscellaneous chairs, an iron bedstead. It smelled stale and damp. On the lower walls grew scalloped shelves of fungus and over the untrod parts of the floor lay a graygreen mold like rotting fur. There was a rattlesnake skin almost the length of the room tacked above the fireplace. The old man watched him watch. I ain't got nary now, he said.

What?

Snakes. I'm out. That'n there was the biggest. Biggest anybody ever seen or heard tell of either.

I wouldn't dispute it, Holme said.

He was eight foot seven inches and had seventeen rattles. Big in the middle to where ye couldn't get your hands around him. Come back here.

They made their way through a maze of crates, piles of rags and paper, a stack of warped and mildewed lumber. Standing in the corner of the room was a punt gun some seven feet long which the old man reached and handed out to him. Holme took it and looked it over. It was crudely stocked with some porous swamp wood and encrusted with a yellow corrosion that looked and smelled of sulphur.

What ye done was to lay it acrost the front end of your skiff and drift down on em, the old man said. You'd pile it up with grass and float down and when ye got to about forty yards out touch her off into the thickest of em. See here. He took the gun from Holme and turned it. On the underside was an eyebolt brazed to the barrel. Ye had ye a landyard here, he said. To take up the kick. He cocked the huge serpentine hammer and let it fall. It made a dull wooden sound. She's a little rusty but she'll fire yet. You can charge her as heavy as you've got stomach for it. I've killed as high as a dozen ducks with one lick countin cripples I run down. They bought fifty cents apiece in them days and that was good money. I'd be a rich man today if I'd not blowed it in on whores and whiskey.

He set the gun back in the corner. Holme looked about him vaguely. On a shelf some dusty jars filled with what looked like the segmented husks of larvae.

You don't pick ary guitar or banjer do ye?

No, Holme said.

If'n ye did I'd give ye one of them there rattles to put in it.

Rattles.

Them snakes rattles yander. Folks that picks guitar or banjer are all the time puttin em in their guitar or banjer. You say you don't play none?

I ain't never tried my hand at it.

Some folks has a sleight for music and some ain't. My granddaddy they claimed could play a fiddle and he never seen one.

None of us never took it up, Holme said.

I'd show ye snakes but I ain't got nary just now. Old big'n yander's the one got me started. Feller offered to give me ten dollars for the hide and I told him I'd try and get him one like it but I didn't want to sell that'n. So then he ast me could I get him one live and I thought about that a little and I told him yes anyways. So he says he'll take all I can get at a dollar a foot and if I come up on anothern the size of old big'n yander he'll give double for it. But I ain't never seen the like of him again. Might if I live long enough. I use a wiresnare on a pole to hunt my snakes with. It ain't good now. Spring and fall is best times. Spring ye can smoke em out and fall they lay around to where ye can pick em up with your hands pret-near. I hunt them moccasins too when I can see one but they don't pay as good and they more trouble. The old man spat into the barren fireplace and wiped his chin and looked about him with a kind of demented enthusiasm.

Well, Holme said, I thank ye for the water and all . . .

Shoo, come out on the porch and set a while. Ye ain't set a-tall.

Well just for a minute.

They went onto the porch and the old man took his rocker and pointed out a chair to Holme. Holme sat and folded his hands in his lap and the old man began to rock vigorously in the rocker, one loose leg sucking in and out of its hole with a dull pumping sound.

You know snakes is supposed to be bad luck, he said, but they must have some good in em on account of them old geechee snake doctors uses em all the time for medicines. Unless ye was to say that kind of doctorin was the devil's work. But the devil don't do doctorin does he? That's where a preacher cain't answer ye. Cause even a preacher won't say they cain't help nor cure ye. I've knowed em to slip off in the swamp theirselves for a little fixin of somethin another when they wasn't nothin else and them poorly. Ain't you?

I reckon, Holme said.

Sure, the old man said. Even a snake ain't all bad. They's put here for some purpose. I believe they's purpose to everthing. Don't you believe thataway?

The old man had leaned forward in his rocker and was watching Holme with an intent look, his thumb and forefinger in his beard routing the small life it harbored.

I don't know, Holme said. I ain't never much studied it.

No. Well. I ain't much neither but that's the way I believe. The more I study a thing the more I get it backards. Study long and ye study wrong. That's what a old rifleshooter told me oncet beat me out of half a beef in a rifleshoot. I know things I ain't never studied. I know things I ain't never even thought of.

Holme nodded dully. I got to get on, he said.

Stay a spell, the old man said. Ain't no need to rush off.

Well, I best get on.

Just stay on, the old man said. I'll learn ye snakehuntin. You look to me like a young feller who'd not be afeared of em.

Maybe, Holme said. But I got to get on.

You got kin over twards the flats?

No.

Ain't married are ye?

No.

Might's well stay on.

The praying minktrapper materialized for him out of the

glare of the sun like some trembling penitent boiling in the heat there, a shimmering image beyond which the shape of the forest rose likewise veered and buckling. He blinked his eyes and stood from the chair. I thank ye kindly, he said, but I got some things needs looked after.

What's that?

Holme was stretching with his hands deep in his pockets, rocking a little on his heels. He stopped. What? he said.

I said what is it needs looked after if it's any of my business.

Holme looked at him. Then he said: I'm huntin a woman.

The old man nodded his head. I cain't say as I blame ye for that. I live to see the fifth day of October I'll be sixty-three year old and I . . .

No, Holme said. My sister. I mean to say I'm a-huntin my sister.

The old man looked up. Where'd you lose her at?

She run off. She's nineteen year old and towheaded. About so high. Wears a blue dress all the time. Rinthy. That's her name.

How come her to run off?

I don't know. She ain't got right good sense in some ways. She just up and left. I don't reckon you've seen such a person have ye?

Not to notice it I ain't.

Well.

I had a wife one time used to run off. Like a dog. Best place to hunt em is home again.

She ain't rightly got a home.

Where'd she run off from then?

Holme had paused with one foot on the top step, one hand spread over his knee. He pursed his lips and spat, dry white spittle. Well, he said, she ain't actual what you'd call run off. She just left. I figured I'd ast anyways. If she might of come this way. If I don't find her soon I'm goin to have to start huntin that tinker and I'd purely hate that.

She got ary kin she might of went to?

No. She ain't got no kin but me.

Kin ain't nothin but trouble noway.

Yes, Holme said. Trouble when you got em and trouble when you ain't. I thank ye kindly.

Shoo, the old man said. Just stay on.

Well, I best get on.

The old man took up his cane from where he had leaned it against the side of the house. Well, he said, come back when ye can stay longer.

I will, he said. He went down the steps into the yard. The hounds raised their eyes to watch him go. He half turned again at the road and lifted one hand and the old man nodded and made a little motion with his cane.

Thank ye for the water and all, Holme said.

Shoo, said the old man. I wouldn't turn Satan away for a drink.

THE TWO HOUNDS rose howling from the porch with boar's hackles and walled eyes and descended into the outer dark. The old man took up his shotgun and peered out through the warped glass of his small window. Three men mounted the steps and one tapped at the door. And who is there? A minister. Pale lamplight falling down the door, the smiling face, black beard, the tautly drawn and dusty suit of black. Light went in a long bright wink upon the knife blade as it sank with a faint breath of gas into his belly. He felt suddenly very cold. The dogs had gone and there was no sound in the night anywhere. Minister? he said. Minister? His assassin smiled upon him with bright teeth, the faces of the other two peering from either shoulder in consubstantial monstrosity, a grim triune that watched wordless, affable. He looked down at the man's fist cupped against his stomach. The fist rose in an eruption of severed viscera until the blade seized in the junction of his breastbone and he stood disemboweled. He reached to put one hand on the doorjamb. He took a step backwards as if to let them pass.

HE KEPT WALKING after the sun was down. There were no more houses. Later a moon came up and the road before him went winding chalky and vaporous through the black woods. Swamp peepers hushed constantly before him and commenced behind as if he moved in a void claustral to sound. He carried a stick with him and prodded each small prone shadow through which he passed but this road held only shapes of things.

When he did reach Preston Flats the town looked not only uninhabited but deserted, as if plague had swept and decimated it. He stood in the center of the square where the tracks of commerce lay fossilized in dried mud all about him, turning, an amphitheatrical figure in that moonwrought waste manacled to a shadow that struggled grossly in the dust.

He hurried on, through the town where houses and buildings in shadow halved the narrow road and his own shape fled nimbly over the roofs, on into the country past farms remote and dark in the lush fields of early summer, the night cool, a hushed blue world of the dead.

Later he slept in a field, trampling a nest out of the fescue and lying there with his hands between his knees, watching the random motes of birds passing across the moon's face in the night.

He was gone in the morning before daybreak. The road went from farmland into pine woods. He walked along with his pockets full of old shelled fieldcorn he had gathered and which he chewed with a grim rotary motion of his jaws. Toward noon he came upon a turpentine camp and he turned in here along a log road until he came to a cluster of sheds. A group of negroes were huddled about on the ground eating cold lunches out of pails and there was a man standing there looking at them or past them, somewhere, one foot propped on a log, tapping with a pencil at a tablet he held. When he saw Holme he stopped tapping and looked at him for a moment and then looked away again. Howdy, he said.

How are you? Holme said.

I ain't worth a shit. You?

Tolerable thank ye. I taken you to be the bossman.

No, I work for these niggers.

Holme sifted the dry corn in his pocket with one hand. I wondered if you might not need some help, he said.

I think I can handle it, the man said. He looked Holme over, the pencil poised in the air. Clark send ye down?

No. I don't know no Clark.

Is that right? I wisht I didn't. The son of a bitch has set me crazy.

Holme smiled slightly. The man turned away, looking

toward the negroes. They were smoking and talking in low voices. He was jotting figures on the pad.

You ain't said, Holme said.

Said what?

If you needed help.

I said no.

I mean no kind of help.

No. Go ast Clark.

Where's he at?

The man looked at him sideways. Are you sure enough lookin for work? he said.

Yessir.

Shit. Well. Well hell, go see Clark anyway. He might can help ye.

Where's he at?

Home most likely. Dinner time. Ast in town.

All right, Holme said. Which way is it?

Which way is what?

Town.

Well which way did you come?

I don't know. I just come up the road and seen this here camp and thought I'd ast.

Well they ain't but one road so if you didn't come thew town it must be on up the road wouldn't you reckon?

Thank ye, Holme said. Much obliged.

The man gave him one last half-contemptuous look and then turned and called something to one of the negroes. Holme went on. A dozen steps on the road he turned again. Hey, he said.

The man looked at him in irascible amazement.

What's that name again? Holme said.

What?

That name. That feller I'm to see in town.

Clark, goddamn it.

Thank ye. He raised a hand slightly in farewell and the man looked at him and shook his head and yelled again at the negroes. Holme went on.

Further on he came to a board culvert through which a small branch sluiced with a cool sucking sound to cross beneath the road. He stood looking down at the water for a moment, then parted the ferns and went into the woods along the branch until he came to a pool. He knelt in the black sand and dipped and spread his hands very white in the clear water, framing his own listing image. From the bib of his overalls he fingered a small piece of soap and a razor in a homesewn leather sheath. He shucked off the straps of his overalls and took off his shirt and began to wash his arms and his chest. With the soap he made a thin and transient lather, honed the razor against the calf of his boot and shaved himself, studying his face in the water and feeling out stray patches of stubble with his fingers. When he had done he splashed water at his face and took up his shirt to dry with before donning it again. He wrapped the soap in a leaf and put it together with the razor in the bib pocket once more and combed his hair briefly with his fingers and rose.

When he did reach town it was past noon, his shirt gone sour again and sweat darkening the white crusts of salt at his sleeves and the cuffs of his trousers which in their raggedness looked blown off to length, tailored by watchdogs. White dust had built upon the wet patches at his knees until he might have knelt in flour and his face and hair were pale with dust save for his eyes which had a smoked look to them. He wandered into the heatstricken square and looked about him, blinking. People were moving from shade to shade beneath the store awnings and across the bright noon clay with leaden steps, moving beneath the blinding heat like toilers in a dream stunned and without purpose. The first man he came upon that was not caught up in this listless tableau was a teamster fitting a wheel. He said him a howdy above his bent back.

Yep, the man said. He ran his forefinger around a tallow tin and brought forth the last of it like cake icing and daubed it over the tapered spline of the axle. Holme watched while he eased the wheel into place and while he fitted the nut and turned it hand tight. He gave the wheel a spin and it went smoothly, dishing slightly and whispering as if it rode through water. Where's that wrench now? he said. He was feeling along the ground and Holme thought for a minute the man was blind.

It's under your foot, he said.

The man stopped and looked up at him, then took up the wrench. Ah, he said, here tis. He tightened the nut and then took the cotterpin from the greasecup where he had put it for safekeeping and bent the ends with his thumb and fitted it and reflared it again. Then he tapped the cup into place with the heel of his hand and rose.

Now, he said, his hands coming clawlike up his overall legs and leaving dark and polished trails of grease, what was it again?

I just wanted to ast ye where I might find a feller named Clark.

Just about any place ye look. County's full of em.

No . . .

Yes tis.

I mean this'n I'm huntin a feller at the turpentine camp out on the road told me to ast for him.

That's the old man I reckon. He's out at Essary's fixin for the auction. They havin a big auction tomorrow.

Holme blinked hugely in the sun and palmed the sweat from his forehead. I'm huntin work, he said.

Are? Don't fall asleep there, you'll tip over and hurt yourself.

Holme squinted his eyes at the man, blinked again at the flat and sunscoured clay about him, turned and started up the street.

The man watched him go for a minute, one elbow propped on the wheel of the wagon. Then he raised his hand in the air. Hey there, he called.

Holme turned.

You, the man said. Hold up a minute.

Holme started slowly back toward him. The man watched him with one hand visored upon his forehead against the sun. You ain't drunk are ye? he said.

No, Holme said. Just a little give out is all.

Are you sure enough lookin for work?

Yessir.

Well, I never meant to be short with ye. I hate to see a feller act whipped though. Damned if I don't. You ain't sick are ye?

No. I ain't sick. You need a man to work?

Well, no. I just thought you looked like you'd had some kind of trouble or somethin. Walkin off thataway. Kindly bothered me. I ain't astin ye your business now.

Everbody's subject to get in a ditch sometime or anothern, Holme said. I ain't lookin for nobody to be sorry for me.

No, the teamster said.

What about this Clark feller?

Now he might have somethin for ye. Why don't ye ast at the store what time they expectin him in. It's a right good ways out there where he's at and I doubt you'd get back against dark.

All right, Holme said. Which store?

Clark's.

Thank ye, Holme said. Much obliged.

That's all right, the teamster said. I hope ye luck.

Much obliged, Holme said again. He nodded and started on up the street and the teamster nodded to him and then to himself more gravely. And say, he called.

Holme turned, still walking.

You talk sharp to that old man you hear?

Holme raised one hand and went on.

The clerk at the store when Holme asked him frowned and said: When you see him comin is when ye can look for him. What is it you wanted with him?

Feller told me to see him about work.

Did?

Two fellers . . .

Well you can wait on him if it suits ye. He may be back directly.

Holme went out and leaned against a stanchion of the porch and watched the people pass and the little dustdevils that went along the road. He dipped up half a handful of corn from his pocket and began to chew it and then he stopped, his face going from vacancy to disgust, and spat the tasteless meal to the ground. As he did so a man rounding the corner leaped back and began to scream at him.

What? Holme said dumbly. What?

Cholera? Cholera?

Hell, it weren't nothin but a mouthful of corn.

I lost a whole family to it now don't lie to me like I ain't never seen it goddamn it.

Shit, Holme said.

O yes. Five youngerns. Five. And damn near the old lady too. God knows why he didn't . . . I taken it back—God knows all right. Why he's kept that flaptongued bitch down here as long as he has. The flowered crown to all other abominations. A walkin plague in your own house. That's what's been visited on me. You sure you ain't sick?

Shit, Holme said. I ain't never been sick a day in my life savin the whoopincough one time.

I'd shoot a man went around with the plague like ary mad dog, the man said.

Ain't nobody plagued, Holme said.

I hope they ain't, the man said. I pray to God they ain't. He came on along the edge of the porch inspecting the damp explosion of chewed corn in the dust there and mounted the steps with a wary cast to his eye. Where's old Clark at? he said. You seen him?

No, Holme said. I'm waitin on him myself.

You sure you ain't a little off your feed? You look kindly peaked to me.

Holme looked at him and looked away, spat, wiped his mouth with the back of his hand. I done told ye, he said.

How long you been waitin on Clark?

Just a little bit. He's out at the auction.

The hell he is. I just come from there. Who told you that?

Clerk in the store here, Holme motioned with his head.

He don't know shit from applebutter, the man said. Where's Leroy?

I don't know no Leroy.

That's right. You ain't from around here, the man said. He lunged wildly at a passing wasp. Get away, goddamn it, he said. Where are ye from can I ast ye?

I ain't from around here, Holme said.

Damn right you ain't, the man said, and went inside.

When he came out again it was with his back to the door in a receding torrent of invective until he stumbled through onto the porch balancing a handful of crackers and a jar of milk, his mouth full, spraying crumbs and oaths into the dim interior for just another minute before he let the door to. Then he sat on the steps and ate and looked up and down the street from time to time and said no more to Holme. Holme was sitting on the edge of the porch with his feet dangling. He was looking the other way when the man did speak. The man said: Yonder comes the son of a bitch.

He watched. The sign in slant green script broken among the parting boards of the wagon's side read Clark Auction Company and rising outsized up from the wagon seat rode a man dressed in a filthy white suit and so huge that the mule and the wagon which carried him looked absurd, like a toy rig in a circus bearing some soiled and monolithic clown. He reined in at the corner of the porch directly in front of Holme, stood in the wagon, adjusted his hat and climbed down. The mule turned its head and looked at Holme and looked away again. The man mounted the steps. The clerk came to the door and opened it for him.

He says he ain't got no butter and tomorrow's Saturday . . .

Shut up and get back in the store, the man said. Howdy Bud, pretty day ain't it? Whew. I was lookin for warm weather to hold off some, wasn't you?

I ain't interested in the weather, the other said. I want to know who's goin to . . .

You know I talked to a feller up the road said he had corn puttin out. What about that?

Aw, you swear he did?—Goddamn it I don't want to hear about somebody's goddamned corn I want them people down out of there.

The big man had removed his hat to peel the sweat from his head with a curled forefinger and now he paused and looked at the other. What people is that, Bud? he said.

Goddamn it you know what people. I ain't havin it. I want shet of em.

And the other, equable, donning again and adjusting his dustcolored hat with the propriety one might a silk derby, saying: Why Bud, you don't reckon I put em there do ye?

I don't care who done it I just want em out of there.

When I wasn't even in town.

I ain't concerned about that. Them two . . .

They on your property.

Yes.

In a tree you said it was?

You know where they're at.

You know the county ain't authorized no facilities for the removal of dead stock.

The other man's jaw was working up and down but nothing came out.

How come you ain't got no butter?

Then it started, an explosion of curses and oaths in such ingenious combinations that the other smiled appreciatively. He turned to Holme and winked. When the man began to run dry and stammer the other put a hand on his shoulder. Easy now Bud, he said. It's a warm day. Tell you what. I'll see what the law can do.

Law's ass. You are the law . . .

Law takes time, the other said. Yours is a unusual case. We don't want to jump too fast here and do the wrong thing, do we? I think maybe another day or so and we'll be able to handle your problem. It's kindly good advertisin for the public peace just now. Ain't it?

Goddamn it I don't care about no advertisin I want them sons of bitches out of my field.

The other was still smiling but his eyes weren't smiling. He said: I believe another day or two, Bud. That'll be all right won't it? He didn't even wait to see what the man would say but lifted his hand and went on in the store. Holme followed him. He didn't look at the man's face standing there when he passed him.

Clark had gone behind the counter and was riffling through bills and notes in a cigar box. The clerk was dusting merchandise. Holme leaned on the counter for a few minutes, the man's huge back to him and his head nodding from time to time, muttering, shuffling the papers, scratching his chin, cursing.

Mr Clark, he said.

Yep.

He didn't turn and Holme didn't speak again and then he did turn, looking at him with a kind of arrogant curiosity. What is it, he said.

Well, I wanted to ast if you might have any work.

You ridin or walkin?

Walkin.

I need a man to circulate handbills but not afoot. Here. Here's one for yourself anyway. He unrolled a thick scroll of printed bills on the counter and peeled one off. Holme took it and looked at it. The bills on the counter recoiled with a vicious slicing sound.

Goin to have the Willis Brothers and Little Aud, Clark said. Free prizes and lemonade. Like to have everbody come.

Yessir, Holme said, looking up. Was they not nothin else

you needed done? A feller said maybe you could use some help. Maybe at the auction . . .

Clark looked at the clerk and the clerk began to dust again and then he looked at Holme. What feller, he said.

Out to the turpentine camp.

What's your name mister.

Holme.

Holme. Where you from Holme.

Holme swallowed and answered very fast. I come from down in Johnson County. I'm just up here huntin work.

You wasn't here Wednesday was you?

No sir. I just come in this mornin.

The man stood there looking down at him and Holme looked about the shelves and their bright labeled wares and then down at the counter.

You know how I hired my deputy, Holme?

No sir.

They was a wagonload of sons of bitches pulled up in a field to pick beans and he's the first'n off the tailgate.

Holme smiled weakly. Clark never had smiled.

You ever been to a auction?

No sir.

He was hefting the weight of the roll of bills in one palm and contemplating Holme. That's the wrong answer, he said. He looked toward the clerk. Where's Leroy?

I don't know. I ain't paid to keep up with him.

Clark lifted an enormous watch from the pocket of his coat and looked at it. Tell you what I'll do, Holme, he said, addressing the face of the watch.

What.

He looked up. You broke, I reckon.

Yessir.

Can you operate a pick and shovel?

I reckon.

All right. See Harold here about gettin you one from back in the back and then go up to the church and dig me two holes. Big enough to put somebody in. And not in the church lot neither. That's all spoke for. These go up in the back where them little markers is at. You might better ast at the preacher's house.

All right, Holme said.

That old pick's loose in the handle to where I'd not trust it, the clerk said.

Is it the heavy trade in here all day that's kept you from mendin it? He turned back to Holme. The county pays a dollar, he said. That's more than I'd pay but I ain't been ast. If you get done this evenin afore dark come by the store here and you can get paid. Otherwise I'll see ye tomorrow. Unless you're still standin here tomorrow waitin on him to get you that pick and shovel.

When Holme came past the churchyard with his shouldered tools there were two negroes there among the stones, one sitting and watching the other and the other naked to the waist and kneedeep in the hole he dug, the pick coming lazily down and ceasing with a small dead thump in the earth. When the seated one saw him he started to rise and then he sat again. The one working stopped and looked up, face shining with sweat, the two of them watching him come along.

Howdy, he said. You sure you diggin in the right place?

Yessir, the seated one said.

You ain't diggin two are ye?

Yessir. I just waitin on him a minute.

Where's the other one?

They ain't but just us.

Holme looked at them blankly. Where's the other hole at? he said.

The two negroes looked at each other. The one digging said: We wasn't told to dig but one.

This'n here is Mrs Salter, the one sitting said, cocking his thumb backward at the stone against which he leaned. He supposed to go on the right cause I ast his right or my right and he say her right.

Holme unloaded the tools from his shoulder and leaned on them and looked about him and then at the negroes again. You mean you ain't diggin but the one hole, he said.

That's all we's told.

It's for somebody else I reckon. You ain't seen the preacher have ye?

I seen him go up the road a little while back.

Holme nodded. To the rear of the church was an untended lot where he could make out some thin board headstones tilted among the weeds. I reckon yander's the place for buryin anybody that ain't spoke for, ain't it?

The one had started to dig again and he stopped but neither answered.

Or ain't it?

Yessir, the one said. I reckon.

Holme nodded to them and went on.

He worked until nightfall and then a little later. He was beginning to feel lightheaded and his empty belly had drawn up in him like a fist. He worked on for a while in the dark and then he quit. There were no lights at the preacher's house. When he got to the store there were no lights there and there was nobody about. He did not know how late it was. He slid the pick and shovel beneath the porch and went on up the road, a solitary figure in that warm and breathing dark, shadowless and unwitnessed. He slept the night in the lee of a hayrick and he woke again before it was light. Before there was any sign or hope of light. Something had passed on the road and he lay huddled against the chill of pending dawn with his arms crossed on his chest in that attitude the living inflict upon the dead and he listened but he could hear nothing. There was something fearful about. He listened for dogs to bark down along the road but no dogs barked. He lay awake a long time and the morning came up in the east in a pale accretion of light heralded by no cock, no waking birds. He rose and went into the road, dusting the chaff from his wretched clothes and stomping his feet in the fine boots now calked with grave earth. He went along toward the town and as he topped a rise in the road two buzzards labored up out of a dead tree in a field from which hung the bodies of three men. One was dressed in a dirty white suit. Nothing moved. The buzzards swung away beyond the woods and there was no sound and no movement anywhere. There was only the gradual gathering of light to which these eyeless dead came alien and unreal like figures wandered from a dream.

He hurried on, into the empty town. It was daylight now. When he got to the store Clark's rig was standing untethered at the corner of the porch with the mule asleep in the traces. He went up the steps and tapped at the door and waited and tapped again. He peered through the window. His silhouette lay on the floor in the bent light. All was dim and dusty with abandonment. He called. After a while he descended the steps into the road again and he stood there and looked all about him and listened for any sound at all but there was nothing. He turned and went on through the town. He was walking very fast and after a while he was running again.

SHE RESTED for a while sitting on the slatted walkway and leaning her aching breasts forward into her hands. The air was dark with gathering rain. A woman went past laden with a feedbag in which something alive struggled mutely. When she spoke the woman gave her an empty look and went on. She rose after a while and went on herself, the dust warm and soft as talc beneath her toes. There were some men standing in front of a store on the other side of the road and they were watching her. She set her shoulders back a little. Then a man came out of a building on the left and crossed in front of her and as he did he tipped his hat, a brief gesture as if swatting idly at a fly. There was a trace of a smile at his mouthcorners.

Hey, she said.

Hey yourself.

She was watching him go on. You ain't a doctor are ye? she called after him.

He stopped and looked back. No, he said. A lawyer. I get the winners, he gets the losers. He was standing in the middle of the road smiling a little, his hand gone to the brim of his hat again.

Well listen, she said, where's they a doctor at?

The lawyer tucked a long forefinger into his waistcoat pocket and fished forth a watch. He snapped it open, looked at it, looked at the sun where it rode darkly as if to verify the hour in that way. He won't be in till about one-thirty, he said. It's ten till now. He snapped shut the watchcase and slipped it into his vest once more. Is it urgent? he said.

What?

Are you in a hurry? His office is in the same building as mine. We sort of mind shop for one another. Right over here. He pointed to a three-storey house with tall windows in the upper part and lettering on the glass.

She looked, brushing back the hair from her face.

What seems to be the trouble? Is it serious? Or were you asking for someone else?

No. It's me.

Yes. Well. Are you sick? I could let you rest in my office until he gets in if you'd like.

She looked across the street toward the house and she looked at the lawyer. I don't want to put ye out none, she said.

No, he said. No trouble. I'm on my way back now.

Well, she said, I would appreciate you showin me where he's at.

Sure, he said. Come along.

She fell in behind him and they crossed the road, her shuffling along rapidly to keep up, watching the backs of his heels, the curved wheeltracks and moonshaped muleprints, until they reached the walkway and on a little further to the building where he stepped to one side and motioned with his hand. After you, he said.

She started up the long dark stairwell, feeling under her naked feet the cold print of nailheads reared from the worn boards. At the top was a small parlor and on either side a door. She turned and looked down at him.

Here, he said. He went past her and set a key in the lock and held the door open for her to enter. Sit down, he said. She looked about, then backed up to and sat in a sort of morris chair with gouts of horsehair erupting from the splayed seams in the leather. She sat with her toes together and her hands in her lap and looked at the floor.

Well, he said. Where do you hail from?

She raised her eyes. He was sitting at his desk, his feet propped into an open drawer, his head bent forward while he held a match to a cigar.

I just come over from acrost the river, she said.

He had been puffing at the cigar and he stopped and gave her a quick look and then went on and got it lit and flipped the match toward an ashtray on the desk. You feel all right? he said.

Tolerable thank ye.

Well the doctor will be along directly.

All right, she said. Listen.

Yes.

I wanted to ast ye somethin afore I seen him.

All right. What is it?

Well, she said. I ain't got but a dollar and I know doctors is costy and what I was wonderin was if he could do me much good for just a dollar.

The lawyer plucked the cigar slowly from his mouth and folded his hands in a coil of blue smoke. I reckon he'll do you at least a dollar's worth, he said. What was your trouble? If you don't mind me asking.

Well, I'd rather just tell him if you don't care.

Yes. Well I'm sure he'll do something for you. He's a good doctor. Anyway we'll know directly.

I don't want to ast no favors from nobody, she said.

Favors?

Yessir. I mean if it's more'n a dollar I'd just as leave not bother him.

He lifted his feet from the drawer and leaned his elbows on the desk. If you need a doctor, he said, it's not too easy to do without. It's not like needing a pair of shoes or . . . she was looking nervously at her feet, one crossed over the top of the other . . . or say a new skillet or something. You just tell him what your trouble is and let him worry about how much to charge. If you don't have but a dollar he might let you pay the rest later on. Or bring him some eggs. Or garden stuff when . . .

I ain't got nary garden, she said.

Well anyway you let him worry about it.

Yessir, she said.

He leaned back again. It was very quiet in the room. The

light waxed and waned and the squatting shape of the windowsash came and went on the wood floor like something breathing. Are you married? he said.

No, she said. Then she looked up and said: I mean I ain't now. I was but I ain't now.

You a widow then?

Yessir.

Well that's a pity. Young woman like you. You got any babies?

One.

Yes.

The room was growing darker. A gust of damp air moved upon them and the frayed lace curtains at the window lifted.

Looks like we're fixing to have some rain, he said.

But it had already started, the glass staining with random slashes, the hot stone ledge steaming.

We get a lot of rain here in the fall, the lawyer said. After it's too late to do anything any good.

They sat in the gathering dark and watched the rain. After a while the lawyer put his feet down again and rose from the chair. That's him now, he said.

She nodded. He went to the door and peered out. She could hear someone stamping and swearing their way up the stairwell.

Looks like you got a little damp there, John, the lawyer said.

The other one said something she couldn't hear.

Well you got one waiting on you.

He looked through the door. A short heavy man with moustaches from which water dripped, peering above the rim of his fogged spectacles. How do, he said.

Hidy, she said.

Just come on in over here. He disappeared and she rose and crossed the floor before the lawyer and gave him a little curtsying nod, ragged, shoeless, deferential and half deranged, and yet moving in an almost palpable amnion of propriety. I sure thank ye, she said.

The lawyer nodded and smiled. That's all right, he said.

When she entered the doctor's office he had his back to the door, shaking out and hanging up his wet coat on a rack. He turned, brushing the dampness from his shoulders, his shirt plastered transparently to his skin there.

Whew, he said. Well now. What was your trouble young lady?

She looked behind her. The lawyer had closed his door. She could hear the rain outside and it was dark enough to want a lamp.

Over here, he said. Take a seat.

Thank ye, she said. She took the chair near his desk and sat, primly, tucking her feet beneath the rungs. When she looked up he was sitting at the desk mopping furiously at the lenses of his spectacles with a handkerchief.

Now, he said. What was it?

Well, it's about my milk.

Your milk?

Yessir. Kindly.

You ain't fevered are you?

No. It ain't that. I mean I don't know. It's my own milk I meant.

Yes. He leaned back and ran one finger alongside his nose, the glasses poised in midair. You're nursing a baby. Is that what it is?

She didn't answer for a minute. Then she said: Well, no. She stopped again and looked up at him for help. He was looking out the window. He turned back and put the glasses on his nose.

All right, he said. First: Are we talking about cow milk or people milk?

People, she said.

Right. Yours?

Yessir.

All right. You have been nursing a baby then.

No, she said. I ain't never nursed him. That's what's ailin me.

You had a baby?

Yessir.

When?

Early of the spring. March I believe it was.

That's six months ago, the doctor said.

Yes, she said.

The doctor leaned forward and laid one arm out upon the desk and studied his hand. Well, he said, I reckon then you must of had a wetnurse. And now you want to know why you never had any milk. After six months.

No sir, she said. That ain't it.

It's not getting any easier, is it?

No sir. They smart a good bit.

You never had any milk.

I never needed none but I had too much all the time.

He looked at the hand as if perhaps it would tell him something and then perhaps it did because he looked up at her and he said: What happened to the baby?

It died.

Of late?

No. The day it was borned.

And you still have milk.

It ain't that so much. I don't mind it. It's that they startin to bleed. My paps.

Then they were both quiet for a long time. The room was almost dark and they could hear the steady small slicing of the rain on the glass and the spat of it on the stone sill. He spoke next. Very quietly. He said: You're lying to me.

She looked up. She didn't seem surprised. She said: About what part?

You tell me. Either about your breasts or about the baby. No woman carries milk six months for a dead baby.

She didn't say anything.

Do you want to show me?

What?

I said do you want to show me? Your breasts?

All right, she said. She stood and unbuttoned the shift at the neck and slid the shoulders down so that she was standing with her arms pinioned in the rotten cloth. It was all she wore.

Yes, he said. All right. I'll give you something for that. It must be very painful.

She worked the dress back over her shoulders and turned to do the buttons. It smarts some, she said.

Have you been pumping them? Milking them?

No sir. They just run by their own selves.

Yes. You should milk them though. Where is the baby?

I don't know. I mean I ain't seen it since it was borned but I believe I know who's got it if I could find him.

And when was it? That it was born.

I believe it was in March but it could of been April.

That's not possible, he said.

Well it was March then.

Look, the doctor said, what difference does it make if it was later than that? Like maybe in July.

I wouldn't of cared, she said.

The doctor leaned back. You couldn't still have milk after six months.

If he was dead. That's what you said wasn't it? She was leaning forward in the chair watching him. That means he ain't, don't it? That means he ain't dead or I'd of gone dry. Ain't it?

Well, the doctor said. But something half wild in her look stopped him. Yes, he said. That could be what it means. Yes.

I knowed it all the time, she said. I guess I knowed it right along.

Yes, he said. Look, let me give you this salve. He swung about in his chair and rose and unlocked a cabinet behind his desk. He studied the interior for a moment and then selected a small jar and closed the cabinet door again. Now, he said, turning and holding up the jar. I want you to put this on good and heavy and keep it on all the time. If it wears off put more. And you'll have to pump them even if it hurts. Try it a little bit first. He slid the jar across the desk to her and she took it and looked at it and sat holding it in her lap.

Come back in a couple of days and tell me how you're doing.

I don't know as I'll be here, she said.

Where will you be?

I don't know. I got to get on huntin him.

The baby?

Yessir.

When did you see it last? You said you never nursed it.

I ain't seen it since it was borned.

Then what was the part you lied about?

Well. About it bein dead.

Yes. What did happen?

He said it was puny but afore God it weren't puny a bit.

And what happened then?

We never had nothin nor nobody.

You're not married are you?

No sir.

And what happened? Was the baby given away?

Yes, she said. I never meant for him to do that. I wasn't ashamed. He said it died but I knowed that for a lie. He lied all the time.

Who did?

My brother.

The doctor leaned back in the chair and folded his hands in his lap and looked at them. After a while he said: You don't know where the baby is?

No sir.

Below them in the street cattle were being driven lowing through the rain and the mud.

Where do you live? the doctor said. What's your name?

Rinthy Holme.

And where do you live then.

I don't live nowheres no more, she said. I never did much. I just go around huntin my chap. That's about all I do any more.

THE ROAD MADE a switchback at the top of the hill and then ran along the ridge so that following it he had a long time to watch the river below him, slow and flat, a dead clay color and wrinkling viscously in the late afternoon light. The road was good until it started down the bluff and then it was washed out again and muddy and plugged with the tracks of mired horses or men or small things that had crossed it in the night. When the road reached the river it went right on into the water and he could see that the water was up. There was a heavy timbered scaffold and a ferrycable running from it out across the river, bellying almost into the current and rising again at the far side. A voice was coming from the far side too but he could not understand what it said. After a while he saw a man come from the ferry and stand on the bank and put his hands to his mouth and then in a minute came the voice again faint with distance. It was just a voice with no words to it. He cupped his own hands to shout but he could think of nothing to shout so he let them fall again and after a while the man went back to the ferry and he couldn't see him any more.

Holme found a dry place in the grass to sit and he watched the river. It was very high and went past with a dull hiss like poured sand. The air had turned cool and the sky looked gray and wintry. Some birds came upriver, waterbirds with long necks, and he watched them. After a while he slept.

When he woke it was growing late and he could see the ferry on the river. What woke him was a horse and when he turned to look there was a man at the landing holding the reins while the horse drank in the river. Holme rose and stretched himself. Howdy, he said.

Howdy, the man said.

You goin acrost?

No, he said. He was watching the ferry.

Holme rubbed his palms together and hunched his shoulders in the cold.

He thinks I am, the rider said.

He does?

Yes. He jerked the horse's head up and ran his palm along its neck. You reckon that's half way, he said.

What's that? Holme said.

The man pointed. The ferry yander. You reckon she's half way here?

Holme watched the ferry coming quarterwise toward them with the snarl of water breaking on the upriver side of her hull. Yes, he said. I allow he's a bit nigher here than yander.

That's right, the man said. Hard to tell where half way is on a river unless you're in the middle of it. He pulled the horse's head around and put one toe in the stirrup and mounted upward all in one motion and went back up the road in a mudsucking canter.

The ferry was the size of a small keelboat. It slowed in the slack shore currents and nosed easily into the mud. The ferryman was standing on the forward deck adjusting the ropes.

Howdy, Holme said.

You still cain't cross. You a friend of that son of a bitch?

Him? No. I was asleep and he come up.

I'm fixin to get me one of them spyglasses anyways, the ferryman said. He came from the barge deck with a little hop and seized up nearly to his knees in the soft mud and cursed and kicked his boots about and made his way to the higher ground. Yes, he said. One of them spyglasses put a stop to that old shit. He was raking his boots in the grass to clean them. He wore a little leather vest and a strange sort of hat that appeared vaguely nautical. Holme chewed on a weed and watched him.

Little old spyglass be just the thing to fix him with, the man said.

What all does he do? Holme said.

The ferryman looked at him. Do? he said. You seen him. Just like that. He does it all the time. Been doin it for two year now. All on account of a little argument. Sends his old lady over to Morgan for him. I ort by rights to quit haulin her fat ass.

Holme nodded his head vaguely.

So anyway you still cain't cross till I get a horse.

All right, Holme said.

People is just a dime. Horses is four bits.

All right.

I cain't afford to make no crossin for no dime.

No. How long do ye reckon it'll be afore a horse comes?

I couldn't say, mister.

I ain't seen many people usin this road.

Sometimes they do and sometimes they don't. It was busy yesterday evenin. I ain't never been more'n a day or two without somebody come along.

Day or two? Holme said.

They be somebody along directly.

I sure would hate to have to wait any day or two.

They ort to be somebody along directly.

It's nigh dark now, Holme said.

They come of a night same as they do of a day, the ferryman said. It's all the same to me. You goin to Morgan?

If it's yan side of this river and in the road I'm goin thew it.

Good little old town, Morgan. Say you ain't never been there?

No, Holme said.

Good little old town, the ferryman said again. He squatted in the grass, looking out over the river. Say you don't aim to lay over there?

No, Holme said. I don't reckon.

Well, I don't ast nobody their business.

Holme sat and crossed the boots before him. He plucked a grass stem and fashioned a loop in one end. It was growing dark rapidly. The river hissing blackly past the landing seemed endowed with heavy reptilian life.

She's still risin, the ferryman said.

Yes.

Say you just goin thew Morgan?

I don't know, Holme said. They any work there?

The ferryman spat and wiped his mouth on his knee. What sort of work? he said.

I don't know, Holme said. He knotted the stem and snapped it. I ain't choicey.

You ain't got nary trade?

No.

I don't know. Might find somethin. Nice enough little old town, Morgan.

Is that your home?

Yep. Borned and raised there. My daddy built this here ferry. I guess you come from over in Clayton County.

No, Holme said.

He could no longer see the ferryman's face and the ferryman didn't say anything for a while. With the dark the river grew louder and Holme wondered if the water was rising or if it was just the dark.

She runs just on the current I reckon you noticed, the ferryman said.

What?

I said she runs on the current if you've not seen such a ferry afore.

No, Holme said. I ain't.

I allowed maybe you'd not. What you do is you snug up

the front and let out the back on a loose line so she noses upriver and the water just pushes her right acrost. Then when ye want to come back you just loose up the snug end and snug up the loose and here she comes.

You don't have to swap ends?

Nope. They both the same. You just change your lines thataway and here she comes.

That's pretty slick, Holme said.

Yes tis. Don't cost nary cent neither.

Did your daddy think it up?

Naw. Folks say he done but he never. He seen one like it somewheres.

It's pretty slick.

Yep. Just change them lines is all they is to it. If you was to set em both the same you wouldn't go nowheres.

No.

Might bust the cable.

Yes.

The ferryman sat down from off his haunches and stretched his feet in the grass. Cable busted once and killed a horse. They said they was a man holdin it and it knocked the horse plumb in the river and left him standin there holdin the reins.

He was lucky, Holme said.

The ferryman nodded. Yes, he said. It wasn't even his horse.

I wish one would come on now, Holme said. I'm gettin cool.

We don't get somebody directly we might ort to have a fire.

I doubt they be much dry wood about.

Well, maybe somebody be along directly.

Yes.

If it was Saturday they'd be here. It's a sight in the world the traffic I get on a Saturday.

What day is it? Holme said.

I don't know, the ferryman said. It ain't Saturday.

They sat in the grass and watched the river run in the dark as if something were expected there. Yes, said the ferryman. She is risin.

Been a sight of rain up here too I reckon.

Yes. Risky to run at night when she's high thataway. Easy to get stove with a tree or somethin.

I guess it would, Holme said.

She scoots acrost like a striped-assed ape when the river's up.

I guess it's up pretty high now.

Yes. Hush a minute.

Holme listened.

The ferryman rose. Here we go, he said.

Is they someone comin?

Listen.

He listened. When the horse came out on the hard ground of the bluff above the river he could hear its hoofs clatter dead along the road, a sound moving sourceless through the dark, no silhouette among the sparse trees of the ridge, no horseman against the night sky. The ferryman had gone to the barge and was making ready to cast off. The rider above them faded out of hearing and Holme knew that he was coming down the road toward the river in the soft mud and after a while he could hear the chink of the horse's trappings and the animal's windy breathing in the dark and then they came out on the landing, visible against the river, the rider leading the horse. He could hear the ferryman say something and the rider said no, and the ferryman said something else and the rider said no again. You've got another fare there.

Holme rose and stretched and made his way across the mud to the ferry. The rider was leading the horse aboard, the horse with knees high and head jerking up nervously and its hoofs clopping woodenly on the ferry deck until the man got him forward and tethered. Holme boarded and got his dime out and handed it to the ferryman. The ferryman nodded and swung his rope and made it fast and the boat began to quiver and to move very slowly out, the eyerings riding on the cable overhead with a rasping sound and water beginning to boil against the hull. The river was dark and oily and it tended away into nothing, no shoreline, the sky grading into a black wash little lighter than the water about them so that they seemed to hang in some great depth of darkness like spiders in a well.

Holme had taken a seat on a bench that ran under the gunwale at the rear of the barge. He reached down and trailed one hand for a moment palmdown in the cold water as if to check his balance. The ferryman was standing riskily on the afterdeck adjusting the ropes. They had begun to move very fast and the water against the upriver hull was raging and he could feel the ferry shuddering under him.

She goes right along, don't she, he called to the ferryman above the howling water, but the ferryman was busy at his ropes, his mariner's cap skewed on his head, watching upward at the cable beneath which they ran and where the rings were now screeching in a demented fiddlenote. At the front of the boat the horse snorted and nickered and clapped one hoof on the boards. When Holme looked back to the ferryman again he appeared to be dancing among his ropes and Holme could hear him swearing steadily. He stood up. They seemed to be in high wind and water was blowing over the deck. The river was breaking violently on the canted flank of the boat, a perpetual concussion of black surf that rode higher until it began to override the rail and fall aboard with great slapping sounds. Holme could no longer hear the ferryman. They were careening through the night wildly. The ferryman leaped to the deck and ran forward. The horse stamped and sidled. The ferryman sprang at the forward ropes. Water was now pouring across the rail and Holme had jumped to the rear capstan where he balanced as best he could and looked about him in wonder. They appeared to be racing sideways upriver against the current. The barge shuddered heavily and a sheet of water came rearward and circled the capstan and fanned with a thin hiss. Then there was a loud explosion and something passed above their heads screaming and then there was silence. The ferry lurched and came about and the wall of water receded and they were drifting in windless calm and total dark.

Holme splashed forward. There was no sound. Ho, he

called. He could see nothing. He felt his way along the gunwale. Something reared up out of the dark before him with a strangled cry and he fell to the deck, scrabbling backwards as the hoofs sliced past him and burst against the planking. He clambered crabwise back along the deck, wet now and very cold. Ho there, he called. Nothing answered. It's tied, he said. But it wasn't tied. When he crossed to the other side he heard it go down the deck and whinny and crash and then he heard it coming back. His eyeballs ached. He dropped to the deck and crawled beneath the rail, up in the scuppers, and the horse pounded past and crashed in the bow. He pulled himself up and started for the rear of the barge and then he heard it coming again. He clawed at the darkness before him, cursing, throwing himself to the deck again while the horse went past with a sound like pistolfire. He waited, his cheek against the cold wood. The barge drifted, swung slowly about, trembling. A race of water wandered over the deck, ran coldly upon him, in his shirt and down his boots and receded again. He could not hear the horse. He could hear the sandy seething of the river beneath him. After a while he rose and started back up the deck. A black fog had set in and he could feel it needling on his face and against his blind eyeballs. When the horse came at him the third time he flattened himself half crazed against the forward bulkhead and howled at it. The horse reared before him black and screaming, the hoofs exploding on the planks. He could smell it. It yawned past him and crashed and screamed again and there was an enormous concussion of water and then nothing. As if all that fury had been swallowed up in the river traceless as fire. The barge rocked gently and ceased. Holme slid to the deck, gasping, his two fists together against his chest. He raised his head and listened to the silence. When he was sure it had gone he rose cautiously and made his way to the bow, unbalanced and staggering in such blackness. With his hands on the rails he leaned and looked down toward the water. The river mouthed the hull gently. After a minute he realized he was standing on something and he reached down to pick it up. It was a boot. He held it in his hands for a moment. Then he leaned and dropped it into the water. The boot tilted and filled and sank instantly as if a hand in the river had claimed it. He felt very cold.

He did not know what to do. He groped his way along to the benches and sat and hugged himself and rocked back and forth. He could hear the whisper of water going up and down over the deck. It sounded as if it were looking for him. After a while he cupped his hands and hallooed into the night. There was not even an echo. His voice fell from his mouth in a chopped bark and he did not call again. He wondered how far away the shore could be, and the dawn.

Once in the night they went through a shoal and he could hear the river going louder until it had risen to a babble and the ferry swung away in a sickening yaw and slid down some rocky flume, him sitting helpless and blind, clutching the bench, his stomach lapsing down black and ropy glides and the fog cold and wet upon him, praying silent and godless in his heart to the river to be easy. They came about in still water and went on. Much later the fog lifted. He rose and watched out over the river. He could see the face of it in sullen and threatful replication and after a while he could see a dark mullioned line of trees. He could not tell how fast they were going, he and this boat. He had not thought of them turning either, but now the graded imprecision of the silhouetted trees swung slowly away into a colorless vapor and went behind him and crept forth again on the far side. And again. They had begun to move faster. When they swung a third time he began to think that they were closer to the trees and now too he could see the pale teeth of a rip in the river near the shore and he could hear it like the stammerings of the cloistered mad. Very soon after this he saw a light. It went away again before he could guess what kind of light it might be but he watched for it. The barge had swung twice more and now he was in eddywater almost beneath the dark wall of trees. He could feel the slide and bump of debris on the hull, the dull grinding of a log sliding under. The light appeared again. A pinflicker set in a glozed cup. He watched. It had begun to rain. He felt it very lightly on his arms and was surprised. He watched the light with his shoulderblades cocked against the chill and the rain falling upon him and soundlessly in the dark upon the peened and seething face of the river.

At first he thought it to be a cabin but it was not a cabin. It had no shape but what it took from breaking on the arch of trees above it and he knew that it was a campfire. The barge had slowed. Some trees passed across the front of the fire and he thought they were men and then a man did cross it, an upright shape that seemed to be convulsed there for a moment before going from sight like something that had incinerated itself. He was very close to the bank now but moving in a slick again and gaining speed.

Ho, he called.

He could see them move. He called again.

Who's there? a voice came back.

He already had a rope up from the bow and in his hand. Now as the barge slid past a last clump of trees there were three men standing on the bank of the river in the gentle rain with the fire behind them projecting their shapes outward into soaring darkness and with no dimension to them at all.

Catch a line, he called to them.

How many of ye is they?

Just me. Here. He couldn't see their faces. He was moving before them and before the light like someone in a stageprop being towed from wing to wing.

You want me to shoot him? a voice said.

Shut up. Thow the line, mister.

He held the line. He was trying to see them but they were only silhouettes. Then the boat began to turn and he could hear the sound of the river again and he threw the line. It uncoiled across the water with a hiss and he could see one of the men move and squat and rise again.

You got it? he called.

Hitch it, one said.

He had swung past them now and no longer could see them at all. He heard the rope saw along the gunwale and tauten and there was a creaking sound as the ferry hove about and he took two little steps to recover his balance. Some tree branches scratched along the hull and broke and came aboard.

Then he was ashore, staving off brush with his arms and making his way through the woods toward the light.

When he entered the little clearing there were only two of them standing there. One was holding a rifle loosely in one hand and picking his teeth. The other stood with long arms dangling at his sides, slightly stooped, his jaw hanging and mouth agape in a slavering smile. The one with the rifle dropped his hand for a moment as if he might be going to speak, but he didn't.

I was on the ferry and it busted loose, Holme said. That's it yander. He pointed vaguely to the darkness. Neither of them looked. They were watching Holme.

You wouldn't care for me to dry a little in front of your fire would ye? I'd be proud to tote wood.

Neither of them spoke. Holme looked about him. The third one was standing just in the rim of light to his left, watching him. He was dressed in a dark and shapeless suit that could not have buttoned across his chest and he wore a shirt with some kerchief or rag knotted at the neck. His face scowled redly out of a great black beard. He jerked his head at Holme. Come up to the fire, he said.

Thank ye, Holme said. I'm wet plumb thew and might near froze to boot.

The other two turned slightly to follow him with their eyes, a predacious curiosity. Holme nodded to them as he passed but they gave no sign of having noticed this.

Set down, the bearded one said, motioning with his hand.

Thank ye, Holme said. He squatted before the fire and

extended his palms over it like some stormy and ruinous prophet. The small rain fell upon them silently and wet wood sang in the flames. The bearded one watched him.

That river sure is up, Holme said.

It is.

Ferryman went overboard.

What ferryman?

Holme looked at him across the fire. The ferryman, he said. The one that was runnin that there ferry.

You ain't the ferryman.

No. I was just crossin the river. We never made it. They was another feller on a horse and I reckon it got him too.

The bearded one was leaning forward with interest. Ah, he said. You ain't the ferryman.

No, Holme said. It knocked him plumb out of his boots. That cable did when it busted. Sounded like a cannonload of cats goin by.

Well now, the bearded one said. I allowed you was the ferryman.

No, Holme said. It was like I told ye.

The bearded one was watching him very intently. He looked down at the fire. On a rock was a pan of black and mummified meat. He watched the fire and rubbed his hands together. The other two men had come up and were squatting half in darkness watching him. The bearded one looked toward them and Holme looked at the pan of meat again.

Help yourself to some meat there if you're hungry, the man said.

Holme swallowed and glanced at him again. In the upslant of light his beard shone and his mouth was red, and his eyes were shadowed lunettes with nothing there at all.

What kind is it?

The man didn't answer.

Holme looked to the fire. I really ain't a bit hungry, he said, but I'd admire to dry this here shirt if you don't care.

The man nodded.

He started to pull the wet shirt off and as he jerked his arms forward he felt the cloth part soundlessly down the back. He stopped and reached behind him gingerly.

Looks like you about out of a shirt, the man said.

Yes, he said. He peeled the shirt from him and looked at it, holding it up before the fire.

You ain't et, the man said.

Holme's stomach turned coldly.

Ain't no need to be backards about it. Get all ye want. We've done et.

He laid the shirt across his knees, reached gingerly and took a piece of the blackened meat from the pan and bit into it. It had the consistency of whang, was dusted with ash, tasted of sulphur. He tore off a bite and began chewing, his jaws working in a hopeless circular motion.

The bearded one nodded. And a rider, he said.

A what? Holme said.

A rider.

Yes.

Ah, he said.

Old crazy horse like to of killed me, Holme said. Whatever it was had swollen in his mouth and taken on a pulpy feel warped and run with unassailable fibers. He chewed.

Where was it you was headed? the man said.

He worked the clot of meat into one cheek. I was just crossin the river, he said. I wasn't headed no place special.

No place special.

No.

Ah, the man said.

Holme chewed. I don't believe I ever et no meat of this kind, he said.

I ain't sure I ever did either, the man said.

He stopped. You ain't et none of this? he said.

The man didn't answer for a minute. Then he said: They's different kinds.

Oh, Holme said.

The one with the rifle across his squatting thighs giggled. Ain't they, he said. Shitepoke, pole . . .

The bearded one didn't say anything. He just looked at him and he hushed.

Ain't no such a thing, he said. Don't pay him no mind, mister. Pull in a little closter there. You Harmon, get some wood.

The one with the rifle rose and handed it to the one who had not spoken and disappeared.

I'd be proud to help fetch some wood, Holme said.

You just set, the man said. You don't need to worry about it.

He chewed.

That is a jimdandy pair of boots you got there, the man said.

Holme looked at the boots. He had sat and they were stretched sideways along the fire, one crossed over the other. They all right, he said.

Yes.

I wisht it'd let up rainin, Holme said. Don't you?

Yes, the man said. What did ye do with the horse?

What horse?

The rider's horse.

I didn't do nothin with him. He like to of killed me. Commenced tearin up and down like somethin crazy till he run plumb off in the river.

More horse than you could, handle was it?

I couldn't even see it.

Or maybe you was afraid to take it. That makes sense.

I don't need no horse, Holme said.

No. Get ye some more meat there.

I still got some, Holme said.

The man turned his head. Harmon had come up with a load of wet limbs and now he dumped them on the ground and knelt in the loamy river soil and began to arrange them before the fire to dry. The man waited. Then he said: Set down. Harmon squatted on his haunches and folded his arms about his shinbones.

Well, the man said, turning to Holme. You've set there and dried and warmed and et but you've not said your name. A feller didn't know he'd think you wanted it kept for a secret.

I don't care to tell it, Holme said. Folks don't commonly ast, where I come from.

We ain't in them places, the man said.

Holme, Holme said.

Holme, the man repeated. The word seemed to feel bad in his mouth. He jerked his head vaguely toward the one with the rifle. That'n ain't got a name, he said. He wanted me to give him one but I wouldn't do it. He don't need nary. You ever see a man with no name afore?

No.

No, the man said. Not likely.

Holme looked at the one with the rifle.

Everthing don't need a name, does it? the man said.

I don't know. I don't reckon.

I guess you'd like to know mine, wouldn't ye?

I don't care, Holme said.

I said I guess you'd like to know mine wouldn't ye?

Yes, Holme said.

The man's teeth appeared and went away again as if he had smiled. Yes, he said. I expect they's lots would like to know that.

Holme wiped his mouth on his naked arm and tried to swallow and then went on chewing. It was very quiet. He listened but he could hear no sound anywhere in the woods or along the river. Not of owl or nightbird or distant hounds.

Some things is best not named, the man said. Harmon

here—he gestured toward the squatting figure—that's his right name. I like for him to set and listen even if he cain't understand much.

Holme nodded.

I like for him to have the opportunity.

Yes.

Harmon did not appear to be listening. He was gazing into the fire like a lean and dirty cat.

He might know somethin and him and me neither one know about it, the man said. Asides I like for him to set there and listen and maybe mend the fire.

Harmon moved. He did not stop looking at the fire but he leaned and groped with one hand until he had hold of some wood and he poked a few pieces into the wasting flames. Holme could see the third one squatting on the far side with the rifle upright between his knees and his face resting against the side of the barrel.

I like to keep the fire up, the man said. They might be somebody else comin.

Holme swallowed the leached and tasteless wad of meat, his eyeballs tilting like a toad's with the effort. I would doubt they was, he said.

The bearded one didn't seem to hear. He stretched his feet forth and crossed them and recrossed them. Holme reached toward the pan before he thought and checked too late. He lifted a sour black chunk of meat and bit into it.

Now these here old boots of mine, the man said, is plumb wore out.

Holme looked at the boots. They were cracked and weather-blackened and one was cleft from tongue to toe like a hoof. He looked at Harmon and he looked at the fire, chewing.

Ain't they? the man said.

I reckon, Holme said. He rearranged the shirt and felt of it.

Get ye some more meat there, the man said.

Thank ye, Holme said. I've a plenty.

Did that ferryman not have nary better shirt than that?

What?

I said did that ferryman not have no better a shirt on him than that?

I never noticed his shirt.

The man watched him. After a minute he turned to Harmon. He says he never noticed his shirt, he said.

Harmon squeezed his shins and giggled and nodded his head up and down.

The man had stretched out before the fire and was propped up on one elbow. He said: I wonder where a feller might find him a pair of bullhide boots like them you got.

Holme's mouth was dust dry and the piece of meat seemed to have grown bigger in it. I don't know, he said.

Don't know?

He turned the shirt again. He was very white and naked sitting there. They was give to me, he said.

They look a mite turned up at the toes, the man said. Did they not know your size?

They was bought for somebody else. He died and I got em give to me is how come they a little big. They all right.

The man shifted slightly and raised one of his own broken

boots and looked at it and lowered it again. Holme could see part of one naked foot within the rent leather.

I reckon a dead man's boots is better than near no boots a-tall, the man said.

He felt cold all over. Harmon raised his head and looked at him and even the one with the rifle that had appeared to be sleeping had now opened his eyes without moving at all and was regarding him with malign imbecility.

You say you was just goin crost the river? the man said.

Holme's voice came out quavering and alien. He heard it with alarm. I was huntin my sister, he said. She run off and I been huntin her. I think she might of run off with this here tinker. Little old scrawnylookin kind of a feller. Herself she's just young. I been huntin her since early in the spring and I cain't have no luck about findin her. She ain't got nobody but me to see about her. They ain't no tellin what all kind of mess she's got into. She was sick anyways. She never was a real stout person.

The man was listening closely but what he said next: I wouldn't name him because if you cain't name somethin you cain't claim it. You cain't talk about it even. You cain't say what it is. I got Harmon to look after him if they do fight. I keep studyin him. He's close, but I keep at it.

Holme stared at him. The man had sat up again and had his legs crossed before him.

He's the one set the skiff adrift this mornin, he said. Even if it just drifted off he still done it. I knowed they's a reason. We waited all day and half the night. I kept up a good fire. You seen it didn't ye?

Yes, Holme said.

How come ye to run your sister off? the man said.

I never.

How come her to run off?

I don't know. She just run off.

You don't know much, do ye?

Holme looked past him and past Harmon to the one with the rifle. He appeared to be sleeping but he wasn't sleeping. He looked at the man again. I ain't bothered you, he said.

I ain't in a position to be bothered.

Holme didn't answer.

That ain't the way it is, the man said.

Holme leaned slightly forward and held his elbows. He could feel the meat weighty and truculent in the pit of his stomach.

Is it? the man said.

No.

Get ye another piece of meat yander.

I've got about all I can hold.

You know, I would think them there big boots would chafe on a feller's heels, the man said.

They all right, Holme said.

I don't believe they are, the man said.

Are what?

All right. I don't believe they are.

Well, it don't make no difference.

When I believe somethin it makes a difference.

Holme watched the fire. In his unfocused vision the coals beaded up in pins of light and drifted like hot spores. Blood had come up in his ears and they were warm and half deaf with it. I don't care, he said.

You will care mister. I think maybe you are somebody else. Because you don't seem to understand me very much. Now get them boots off.

Harmon looked up and smiled. Holme looked at the man. The fire had died some and he could see him better, sitting beyond it and the scene compressed into a kind of depthlessness so that the black woods beyond them hung across his eyes oppressively and the man seemed to be seated in the fire itself, cradling the flames to his body as if there were something there beyond all warming. He reached and slid the boots from his feet, one, the other, and stood them before him.

Harmon, the man said.

Harmon rose and came for the boots and took them to the man. The man seized them and examined them, bending closer to the fire, turning them in his hands like some barbaric cobbler inspecting the work of another world. He pulled off his own boots and put on these new ones and stood in them and took three steps up and two back and turned. Harmon had gathered up the old boots and was putting them on. The one with the rifle watched happily.

All right, the bearded one said.

Holme squatted with his naked feet beneath him.

Fix his, the man said.

Harmon carried the boots he had discarded to the one with the rifle and stood them before him. The one with the rifle looked at them and looked up at Harmon. Harmon took the rifle from him and kicked at the empty boots.

Do em for him, the man said.

Harmon knelt and pulled off the nameless one's boots and pushed the other boots at him. Then he rose with these boots and turned. The man gestured.

Holme watched, squatting shoeless and half naked. Harmon came toward him smiling, the rifle in one hand and the last pair of boots in the other. He dropped them alongside Holme and stood looking down at him. Holme looked at the bearded one.

Them's for you, the man said.

Holme looked at them. They were mismatched, cracked, shapeless, burntlooking and crudely mended everywhere with bits of wire and string. He looked at the nameless one who sat likewise barefoot with a pair of boots before him. Relieved of the rifle his hands lay on the ground on either side of him and he was watching Holme. Holme looked away.

I said them ones there is yourn, the man said.

Holme looked at the boots again, then took one up slowly and pulled it onto his foot. A sour reek welled out of the top.

You don't have much to say, do ye? the man said.

No.

I guess you think maybe you and me should of traded.

I don't care, Holme said.

I believe in takin care of my own, the man said. That's the way I think.

Ever man thinks his own way, Holme said.

Leave him alone Harmon.

Harmon stepped away from him. Sometime it had stopped raining. Holme hadn't noticed. He had not felt the rain on his naked back, the small rain that died in the fire soundlessly.

You may see the time you wish you had worse, the man said.

Holme made a small helpless gesture with one hand.

Where was you headin sure enough?

Nowheres, Holme said.

Nowheres.

No.

You may get there yet, the man said. He came along the edge of the fire and stopped, looking down at Holme. Holme could see only his legs and those of Harmon a little further beyond. The fire had burned low and there was but a single cleft and yellow serpent tongue of flame standing among the coals. A third pair of boots came up and Holme looked at them. They stood slightly toed in and on the wrong feet.

That ain't all, is it? the man said.

I ain't got nothin else, Holme said.

The man spat past him into the fire. Somethin else, he said. Have you got a sister sure enough?

I done told ye.

Run off with some tinker.

Yes.

She ain't here to tell it her way. Is she?

No.

And where do you reckon they've got to by now?

I don't know.

Just further on down the road. Don't you reckon?

Yes. I reckon. I ain't studied it.

Ain't studied it.

No.

He seemed to be speaking to the fire. When he lifted his head he could see the three of them standing there watching him, ragged, filthy, threatful.

Yes, the man said. You've studied it.

Holme didn't answer. He turned his face to the fire again.

Harmon, the man said. Leave him be.

Holme didn't look up. He heard their steps receding out of the firelight among the wet leaves toward the river where the ferry was tied. He had the shirt clutched in both hands and was staring in mute prayer at the wand of flame that trembled before him so precariously and he did not move at all. Then he heard steps coming back. He lifted his head. Harmon came smiling out of the dark like an apparition. He did not have the rifle. He did not have anything in his hands. He slouched toward Holme and bent over him. Holme recoiled. Harmon didn't seem to notice. He took up the pan and tilted the remaining meat into the fire and clicked the pan against a rock and stepped back and turned and was gone. Holme could see one of the chunks in the bright coals. It lay there soundless as stone and apparently impervious to flame. He did not move. He listened for their voices but he could hear nothing. After a very long time he could hear the river again and even though the fire had died he did not move. Later still he heard a mockingbird. Or perhaps some other bird.

THE MUD IN the road had cured up into ironhard rails and fissures which carts and wagons had cloven in the wet weather past and the tinker's cart bobbled drunkenly among them with the tinker shackled between the shafts and leaning into the harness he had devised for himself. He was looking at nothing other than the road beneath him and when the girl spoke to him he started in his traces like one wrenched from a trance and halted and looked about. She was seated by the roadside on a stone and she wore some lateblooming wildflower in her pale hair.

Howdy little mam, he said. How you?

Tolerable, she said. You the tinker used to go over in Johnson County some?

They Lord honey I ain't been over there in six or eight months. Are you from over thataway?

Yes, she said. You ain't got nary cocoa have ye.

No, he said, I ain't. I don't get enough call for it to mess with totin it. I got coffee.

And you stocks them books.

What books?

Them pitcher books for the men. Them books.

The tinker's eyes shifted warily. Who are you? he said.

I'm the mother of that chap you got.

I ain't got no chap, the tinker said.

I want him back, she said.

You don't see him do ye?

What have ye done with him.

I ain't got him.

She had not moved from the rock. She smoothed the ragged dress down over her knees and looked up again. I want him, she said.

The tinker was now standing more easily between the cart shafts, watching her with interest and with something else in his little goat's face. How you know I got him? he said.

You got him off my brother, she said. I got to get him back.

How old a chap is it? This'n you claim to of lost.

He ain't but about eight months.

Eight months. And how long you been missin him?

All that time.

The tinker spat lazily over his forearm where it hung by a thumb in the bib of his jumper and drew down one eye cunningly. That sure is a long time, he said. I would hate to be in ary such fix as that.

I hate it myself, she said.

All that nurse fee.

That what?

Nurse fee addin up all the time. Most likely comes to a right smart.

I never thought about that, she said.

No, the tinker said. I allowed maybe you'd not.

I ain't got no money.

No money.

No.

Well. Course even did I know the whereabouts of it they wouldn't be no way tellin it was yourn. Just your word is all.

I wouldn t want it if it wasn't mine.

Well now I don't know. Some women is a fool about a youngern. Do anything to get one.

I just want what's mine.

Maybe you the kind of gal fool enough about a youngern to do anything to get one.

No, she said. He's mine sure enough.

Well, said the tinker. Wouldn't do nothin much to get one eh?

This'n I would, she said. I want him back.

Well now, said the tinker.

I'll work out that fee or just whatever, she said.

The tinker watched her, his thumbs still hooked in his jumper. Well now, he said. You right sure about that?

Yes, she said. I got to have him back.

The tinker shrugged his patched jacket higher onto his shoulders and gripped the cart shafts. Well, he said, if you ain't got nothin else to do just come along with me.

He started off and she fell in behind and padded after him, shoeless and tattered, watching the cart lurch and weave and the tinware hung from the travis poles swing in mounting discord like a demented symphony. They went down the road the way she had come.

They went past houses and along fenced fields where late corn stripped of fodder stood naked and grotesque out of the dead scrub weeds and the intermittent bright shapes of pumpkins. The cart went along on its camshaped wheels like a crippled dog. The tinker did not speak. Yellow leaves were falling in a field and lay already deep in the stony troughs a last crude harrowing had left. She walked looking down at her feet and her lips were moving slightly. The sound of the tinker's cart faded to the drowsy clangor of belled cattle before she looked again and saw him far down the road. She hurried to catch up, holding her dress tight in one fist between her breasts and the cloth already dark with milk.

For the rest of the day she followed behind the cart as if tethered to it. The tinker did not speak nor did he look back and he seemed to have no need of rest. They went through the late afternoon curiously processional and grave among the banded shadows, the tinker stooped in the rotted leather with his cap far back on his head and eyes to the ground and her caught up in the wake of the cart and its lonely tolling tinware like some creature rapt and besorced by witches' music, demon piping.

Come evening the tinker left the road and turned up a weedy wagon path, giving her a brief look backward and motioning with his head. They climbed up through a field, the cart badly tilted and the tinker near horizontal in the harness. When they came to the top of the hill the track turned and they went on in blue dusk through a high meadow out of which sprang small fowl to wheel away with indignant cries over the sedge. At the end of this meadow was a cabin.

They pulled up in the dooryard and the tinker unbuckled himself from out of his traps and set the cart down. She came along slowly and looked in through the halfopened door. Weeds grew at the threshold and from inside came a musty smell.

They ain't nobody here, she said.

No, he said. Come in.

She followed him uncertainly into the gloom and stood looking about her. From the naked sash of a window on the far side a dead light fell through looped and dusty skeins of cobwebbing and laid upon the plumbless floor a pale and bent mandala.

Ain't they nobody here? she said.

No.

What all did we come for?

Come in, he said. Ain't no need to stand there like a orphan.

She came slowly to the center of the room and stood in the fading patch of light like one seeking warmth of it or grace. A faint stale wind was coming through the window and she turned her face there and breathed deeply. The tinker traversed the room with gnomelike stealth, still bowed in his posture of drayage.

Set down, he said.

She could see no place to sit. She turned and spoke into the gloom after him: He ain't here.

No, he said. A match flared rich sulphurous light in which the tinker's malformed shape turned quavering, faded and expired. Not here, he said.

She went to the window and looked out. The ground fell away to a branch where willows burned lime green in the sunset. Dark little birds kept crossing the fields to the west like heralds of some coming dread. Below the branch stood the frame of an outhouse from which the planks had been stripped for firewood and there hung from the ceiling a hornetnest like a gross paper egg.

The tinker returned from the cart with a lantern and placed it upon the mantel and lit it. She watched him. He had a jar of whiskey beneath one arm and he knelt in the floor before the hearth like some sackclothen penitent. He was breaking small brush and sticks and soon there was a flame to which he bowed prone and blew gently upon. He sat back on his heels and coaxed the fire with his wafted cap. You ain't took root there have ye? he said.

She moved across the empty cabin toward the door and stood there for a moment and then closed it. On the back of it hung a coat cocooned in spiderweb like some enormous prey and on the floor lay a dead bird. She toed it with her naked foot. Spooned to a shell, faintly soursmelling. A small white grub writhed in the damp spot it left. She took down the flower from her hair and held it at her breast and turned. The tinker had the jar of whiskey aloft before the lantern. He unscrewed the lid, paused a moment as if to take breath, and drank. She watched his slack throat pump and his eyes tighten. He lowered the jar again and said Whoof and clapped the lid back on as if something might escape. When he saw her watching he extended the jar in one hand. Drink? he said.

I don't care for none, she said.

No. He turned and set the jar beside the lantern. His sparse gray hair stood about his head electrically and in all these gestures before the fire he looked like an effigy in rags hung by strings from an indifferent hand. Come over by the fire till ye warm, he said.

I ain't cold.

The tinker was not looking at her. I expect you're hungry, he said.

She didn't answer for a minute. Nor did he turn his head. Yes, she said.

He left the fire and crossed the room and went out. When he came in again he had a small willow hamper over one arm and a load of wood. She had come to the fire and was standing with her back to it. He set the hamper on the floor and stacked the wood.

They used to be a table but I burnt it for firewood oncet of a cool evenin, he said.

She nodded.

Set down, he said. I got some cold supper.

He had squatted on the floor and opened the hamper. She sat carefully with her legs tucked.

Here, he said. Get ye a piece of this cornbread.

She took a chunk of the bread and bit into it. It was hard and sandy and tasteless.

Get ye some of these here beans.

She nodded, her mouth stuffed. He was dipping up beans

out of a bowl with a piece of the cornbread. Get all ye want, he said.

Is it far to where he's at? she said.

Far and far, said the tinker.

She scooped up some beans on her bread and crammed it into her mouth, flicking crumbs from her lap, her streaked and dusty feet tucked beneath her. When do we get there? she said.

The tinker looked at her. We, is it? he said.

I guess we fixin to get a early start of the mornin ain't we?

It's a hard thing to know what daylight will bring any day, the tinker said. Get ye some more cornbread there.

I've got all I need.

Ain't much of a big eatin gal are ye?

I'm some out of the habit.

Ah, the tinker said.

You reckon we'll get there tomorrow sometime?

Tomorrow?

Will we?

The tinker chewed steadily. Over the floor their long flung shadows swayed like dancing cranes. Little sister, he said, you ain't the first slackbellied doe to go about in the woods with them big eyes.

I just want my chap, she said.

Do ye now?

You said I could work it out.

They's work and they's work, the tinker said. He rose to his knees and reached down the whiskey and set it before him.

I'll do just whatever, she said. I ain't got nothin else to do.

The tinker smiled and captured the beanbowl between his thin shanks and wiped up the remnants with the last of the bread. He chewed with eyes half closed and his face by the firelight hung in a mask of morbid tranquillity like the faces of the drowned.

You don't need him, she said.

He wiped his wattled chin with his cuff and took up the jar and drank. He was watching her very steadily above the rim. He set the jar down and recapped it. I've gone up and down in this world a right smart, he wheezed, and I've seed some curious ways. But I never to this day seen a stout manchild laid out in the woods save one.

Woods? she said.

They don't nourish out of the earth like corn.

He was give to ye. Was he not give to ye?

He was not give to nobody.

What did ye have to give for him?

Yes, the tinker said. What did I have to give for him.

I'll make it up to ye, she said. Whatever it was.

Will ye now, said the tinker.

I'll work it out, she said. I can work if I ain't never had nothin.

Nor never will.

Times is hard.

Hard people makes hard times. I've seen the meanness of humans till I don't know why God ain't put out the sun and gone away.

Whatever it was you give, she said softly. I'll give it and more.

The tinker spat bitterly into the fire. They ain't more, he said.

You promised.

I promised, the tinker said. I promised nothin.

He's mine, she whispered.

The tinker looked at her. She had both thumbs in her mouth. Yourn, he said. You ain't fit to have him.

That ain't for you to judge.

I've done judged.

She had leaned forward and her eyes were huge and hungered. She touched his ragged sleeve with two fingers. What did ye give? she said. I'll make it up to ye. Whatever ye give. And that nurse fee.

The tinker jerked his arm away. He leaned his face toward her. Give, he said. I give a lifetime wanderin in a country where I was despised. Can you give that? I give forty years strapped in front of a cart like a mule till I couldn't stand straight to be hanged. I've not got soul one in this world save a old halfcrazy sister that nobody never would have like they never would me. I been rocked and shot at and whipped and kicked and dogbit from one end of this state to the other and you cain't pay that back. You ain't got nothin to pay it with. Them accounts is in blood and they ain't nothin in this world to pay em out with.

Let me have him, she moaned. You could let me have him.

Let you have him, the tinker sneered.

I'd care for him, she said. They wouldn't nobody like me.

Like you done?

He done it. I never.

Who? the tinker said.

My brother. He's the one.

Yes, the tinker said. He's the one would of laid it to early rest save my bein there. Cause I knowed. Sickness. He's got a sickness. He . . . the tinker stopped. It was very quiet in the cabin. They could hear the branch murmuring. Or perhaps it was the wind. The tinker stopped and stared at her with his viper's eyes gone wild in their black wells. It ain't hisn, he said.

It ain't nothin to you.

The tinker leaned and seized her wrist in his boney grip. It ain't, he said. Is it?

Yes.

Neither of them moved. The tinker did not turn loose of her arm. That's a lie, he said.

What do you care?

That's a lie, he said again. You say it's a lie.

She didn't move.

You say it's a lie now, the tinker said.

You don't want him, she whispered. You wouldn't of took him if you'd of knowed . . .

The tinker pulled her close. You say that's a lie damn you.

It's no right child, she said. You don't want him. Her body was contorted with pain and her eyes closed.

Yes, said the tinker. You'd try it wouldn't ye? You lyin little bitch. He flung her arm back and she crumpled up and held it in her other hand. The tinker rose and stood gaunt and trembling above her. You'll see me dead fore ye see him again, he said.

You won't never have no rest, she moaned. Not never.

Nor any human soul, he said.

The fire had died to coals. The tinker swung down the lamp and their shadows wheeled wildly from each other and froze on opposite walls. Don't foller me, the tinker said. You foller me and I'll kill ye.

She didn't move.

Bitch, he said. Goddamn lyin bitch.

She had begun to keen softly into her hands. The tinker could hear it a long way down the road.

He could hear it far over the cold and smoking fields of autumn, his pans knelling in the night like buoys on some dim and barren coast, and he could hear it fading and hear it die lost as the cry of seabirds in the vast and salt black solitudes they keep.

HOLME WALKED across the stony earth with his eyes on his broken boots, crossing a black and fallow bottom newly turned, the wind coming very steady and cold and with it like pieces of scaled slate martins with shrill chittering cast up motionless to break and wheel low along the ground past him once again. When he reached the fence he stopped for a moment to look back at the road and then he went on, crossing into a field of rank weeds that heeled with harsh dip and clash under the wind as if fled through by something unseen.

He stood before the cabin uncertainly, his palms resting in the small of his back. He looked toward the road again. Then he mounted the steps to the porch and crossed and entered through the open door.

It was a very old cabin and the ceiling of the room he stood in was little higher than his head, the unhewn beams smoked a foggy and depthless black and trellised with cobwebbing of the same color. The floor was buckled and the walls seemed tottering and he could see nothing plane or plumb anywhere. There was a small window mortised crookedly into the logs of one wall, the sash hung with leather hinges. That and the long clayless chinks among the logs let in the waning light of this day and wind crossed the room with the steady cool pull of running water. There was a claymortared fireplace of flatless and illfitted fieldstone which bulged outward in the room with incipient collapse, a wagon spring for lintel, the hearth of poured mud hard and polished as stone. A serpentine poker. Two wooden bedsteads with tickings of husks and a halfbed with a mattress on which lay curled a dead cat leering with eyeless grimace, a caved and maggoty shape that gave off a faint dry putrescence above the reek of aged smoke. He took hold of the mattress and pulled it from the bed and dragged it to the door, fighting it through the narrow opening and outside and long bright red beetles coming constantly from beneath the cat to scatter in radial symmetry outward and drop audibly to the floor. He threw the mattress in the yard and went back in. In the kitchen a doorless woodstove propped in the front with two bricks against the floor's fierce incline. A partitioned mealbin with sifter and a hard dry crust of meal adhering to the wood, the meal impregnated with worms whose shed husks littered the floor of the bin among micedroppings and dead beetles. A solid butternut safe in which languished some pieces of cheap white crockery, chipped and handleshorn coffeecups, plates serrated about their perimeters as though bitten in maniacal hunger, a tin percolator in which an inverted salmoncan sat for a lid. A nameless gray dust lay over everything. He returned to the front room and at the bed pressed one spread palm down in the center of the ticking and looked about him wearily.

Later he went out and gathered wood. He found beanpoles in a log crib behind the house and brought them in and he found some roughsawn chestnut boards. When he had got the fire going he pulled one of the beds up toward the hearth and sat down and watched the flames. Smoke seeped from under the wagon spring and stood in blue tiers and he could hear swifts in the flue fluttering like wind in a bottle. He sat on the bed with his hands dangling between his knees. The window light had crept from the floor onto the far wall and the room lay traversed with a bar of bronze and hovering dust. After a while he rose again and went out for more wood.

When he came back he built up the fire and pulled off the stinking boots and stretched out on the bed. There was a string of dried peppers hanging from a nail in the beam over the fireplace. They looked like leather. In the chimney's throat frail curds of old soot quivered with the heat. A deermouse came down from somewhere in the logs, soundless as a feather falling, paused with one foot tucked to his white bib and regarded him with huge black eyes. He watched it. He blinked and it was gone. He slept.

He was cold all night and in the morning when he woke there was a frost. There was also a man watching him with one bright china eye from behind the paired bores of a shotgun.

Get up, he said.

Holme sat slowly.

Now get your boots. He motioned sideways with his head to where they lay in the floor.

He bent to reach for the boots and got one up, fumbling at it with his naked foot.

Hold it, the man said, waving the barrels in an arc before his face.

He stopped, holding the boot up, watching the man.

Just tote em with ye.

He got the other boot and sat there in the bed holding them in his lap.

Now let's go, the man said, stepping back and motioning toward the door with the shotgun.

He rose and crossed the floor and stepped out. The long flat grass about the house was blanched with frost, the barren landscape beyond sprayed with those small and anonymous birds of winter. He had not thought of such cold weather and was surprised to see it come.

Let's go, the man said.

He descended the rimed planks and stood barefooted in the yard. The man came down the steps waving the barrels at him. They crossed through the frozen grass to the fence and then across the iron clods and furrows of the plowed land and into the road.

Gee, the man said.

Holme looked at him.

The man waved the barrels to the right and he tucked the boots up under his arm and turned down the road, advancing upon his lean and dancing shadow with feet that winced in the cold sand. He could hear behind him the measured tread of the armed man, and after a while his breathing, but the man spoke no word. The sun was gaining and he could feel it a little on his back and it felt good.

When they had gone a mile or better along the road they came to a wagon road that went off to the right.

Here ye go, the man said behind him.

He turned up the road. It was washed out and weed-grown and with the mounting sun water had begun again over the bare stones in the gullies. They climbed on, past high oblique faults of red sandstone, coming at last into a field where the road leveled.

Just hop on down, friend, the man said. Tain't far now.

They came past a barn and beyond that a frame house mounted at the corners on high cairns of rock. A row of chickens regarded them from the porch.

Ho Squire, the man called out, hallooing along his raised palm. Hold up right here, he said to Holme. He advanced to the porch and rapped on the floor. Ho there, he called.

Come up, said a woman's voice from the house.

Go on, the man said.

Holme shifted the boots to the other arm and mounted onto the porch past the chickens and went in. He could smell breakfast cooking.

On back, the man said.

He crossed the room and went through the door at the far side. The woman was coming in carrying an empty pail. She said Howdy without looking at them and went into the kitchen. They followed her. There was a man sitting at the table eating eggs and biscuits from a large platter before him and as they entered he looked up at them. He was dressed in his undershirt, a verminous-looking bag of ashgray flannel from which the sleeves were gone at the elbow as if chewed off. He turned back to his plate before speaking.

Mornin John. Been huntin?

Huntin housebreakers, the man said.

Have eh?

Yep. He poked Holme forward with the shotgun.

This him? he said, not looking up, spooning eggs sideways onto his fork and into his mouth, his chin almost resting on the table.

I caught him in daddy's old house a-layin in the bed.

How'd he get in.

How'd you get in, the man said.

I come thew the door, Holme said.

He come thew the door.

Did eh?

He was a-layin in the bed.

The seated squire nodded, wiping up grease from the platter with a large biscuit. I don't drink coffee or I'd offer ye some, he said, leaning back and wiping his mouth with the palm of his hand. Now, what was your name young feller?

Culla Holme.

You a indian?

No sir.

What was your first name.

Just Holme is my last name. Culla. Holme.

Well, the squire said, say you broke in John's daddy's old house?

I never broke in, I just come in. It wasn't locked nor nothin. I didn't know nobody lived there. They wasn't nothin there to let on like it.

They's furniture, the man with the shotgun said. You was a-layin up in the bed your own self.

They was a dead cat in the othern, Holme said.

I never seen it, he said. He turned to the squire. He thowed the beddin out in the yard for it to rain on. I wasn't goin to tell that.

If that would of done it here back in August I'd of hired him to tote everthing I got outside, the squire said.

It had a old dead cat layin in it, Holme said.

All right, hush now, the squire said. Holme. That's it ain't it?

Yessir.

Where do you come from Holme?

I come from down in Johnson County.

What did they run you off for down thataway.

They never run me off.

Well what are you doin up here?

I was huntin work.

In John's daddy's old house?

No sir. I just wanted to lay over there.

Did you have a sign out up there for hirin hands John?

John smiled cynically, the gun cradled in the crook of his arm. Not to my recollection, he said.

No, the squire said. He leaned back in his chair and drummed his fingers four times on the table edge and looked up at Holme.

Well Holme, how do you plead?

Plead?

Guilty or not guilty?

I ain't guilty.

You wasn't in John's daddy's old house?

I was in there but I never broke in.

Well. Maybe we can make it just trespass then.

Holme looked at the man and the man looked back at him. The squire was tapping his fork idly against the edge of the empty plate and sucking his teeth.

I don't figure I done nothin wrong, Holme said.

Well if you want to plead not guilty I'll have to take you over to Harmsworth and bind ye over in custody until court day.

When is that?

The squire looked up at him. About three weeks, he said. If they don't postpone ye. If you get postponed it'll be another six weeks after that. And if you get . . .

I'll take the guilty, Holme said.

The squire leaned forward and pushed away the plate. Right, he said. Guilty. He took up a piece of cornbread from a bowl of it in the center of the table and fell to buttering it. Ethel, he said. Hey, woman.

She came in with a small oak box and set it on the table.

Guilty of trespass, the squire said.

She was fumbling among keys that hung to her by a string.

When she got the box open she took out some forms and a quill and inkstand. What's his name? she said.

Give her your name, the squire said.

Culla Holme.

What?

Culla Holme.

How do you spell it? She was sitting at the end of the table with the quill poised above a document.

I don't know, he said.

He don't know how to spell it, she said.

The squire looked at her and then he looked at Holme. His mouth was full of cornbread. Put somethin down, he said. You can guess at it, cain't ye?

No sir. I ain't never . . .

Not you.

Yessir.

Say it once more slow, she said.

He said it.

She wrote something. What was it now, she said, turning to the squire.

You got his name?

Yes. What was it now?

Housebreak . . . No. What was it? Trespass? Trespass. He kicked a chair. Here John, set down. You makin the place look untidy.

John sat. There was no sound in the room save the scratch of the pen. Holme stood before them shifting from one foot to the other.

All right, she said.

You ain't forgot the date have ye? Like you done on some of them last'ns.

No, she said.

All right.

She turned the paper around and made a little X at the bottom and held the quill toward Holme. He took it and bent above the paper and made an X beside the X and handed back the quill. She signed it and wafted it in the air for a moment and handed it to the squire. He waved it away with a languorous hand and looked at Holme.

I fine ye five dollars, he said.

I ain't got no five dollars.

The squire blew his nose into a stained rag and put the rag back in his hip pocket. Ten days then, he said. You can work it out.

All right.

Set down. He turned to the woman. Put that up now and get him some breakfast. You had breakfast? No. Get him some breakfast. Cain't work prisoners on a empty stomach. All right John, was that all it was you wanted?

John was sitting forward in his chair waving one hand about. Just a danged minute, he said.

What is it?

Well dang it, how many of them ten days does he work on my place?

The squire had paused with his hand outstretched, scratching at something in his armpit. Your place? he said.

My place.

Why would he be comin down to work on your place?

Well dang it I brought him in. He was breakin in my daddy's house . . .

I cain't be comin down to your place with him ever day just because he happened to pick your daddy's old house to break into.

Well if I hadn't of arrested him he'd not be here a-tall . . .

I appreciate you bringin him in and all, John, but they ain't no reward out for him nor nothin. Is they now? I don't make the law, I just carry it out.

Well I don't see why you ort to benefit from what I done. Or from what he ain't able to pay. I guess you goin to pay back the county his wages, or fine, or whatever . . .

The squire had stopped scratching. Well now John, he said, you know my books is open to anybody. Ain't that right, woman.

That's right, the woman said. Holme was watching her. She wasn't listening to any of it.

It wouldn't hurt you none to let me have him a few days out of them ten.

The squire shook his head wearily. John, he said, you and me has always been good neighbors. Ain't we.

I reckon, John said.

Have I ever turned ye down for a favor?

I ain't never ast ye none.

Well you always knowed all you had to do was ast. Ain't that right?

That's right, the woman said. The squire threw her a sharp look.

I don't know, John said. Ain't this a favor?

No.

No. It's just what's fair.

Don't make no difference about fair or not fair, it's against the law. You ain't authorized to work no prisoners.

I ort to of just shot him and let it go.

No, you done right bringin him in like ye done. But you cain't ast me to break the law and turn him back over to ye. Can ye now?

Shit. Scuse me mam.

I wouldn't ast you to break the law. Would I now. John?

John had risen from the chair. He didn't look back. He went out through the house with the shotgun hanging in one hand and his boots exploding over the bare boards through the rooms and they could hear the doorlatch and then the loud and final closing of the door and silence again for a moment and then a riotous squabble of chickens and then nothing.

Set down, the squire said. What are you doin with your boots off of such a cold mornin?

Holme took the chair the other man had vacated and sat and pulled on the boots laboriously. He stamped his numb feet on the floor but he could feel nothing. He looked up.

He told me to just tote em. I reckon he figured a feller barefoot be less likely to cut and run.

The squire shook his head sadly. I believe he's slipped a cog somewheres, he said.

I never bothered nothin in his old house, Holme said.

Don't make no difference, the squire said. You done been sentenced. I give ye pretty light for a stranger anyways.

Holme nodded.

We'll get you started here directly you get your breakfast.

Thank ye, Holme said.

Don't thank me. I'm just a public servant.

Yessir, he said. Grease was frying violently in a skillet behind him and the woman was putting biscuits to warm in the oven. His stomach felt like it was chewing.

The old lady'll fix ye a bed here in the kitchen. You ain't no desperate outlaw are ye? Ain't murdered nobody?

No sir. I don't reckon.

Don't reckon eh? The squire smiled.

Holme wasn't smiling. He was looking at the floor.

Get ye fattened up a little here on the old woman's cookin you'll be all right, the squire said. Might get some work out of ye then. You reckon?

Yessir. I ain't scared to work.

The squire had tilted back in his chair, regarding him. I don't believe you're no bad feller Holme, he said. I don't believe you're no lucky feller neither. My daddy always claimed a man made his own luck. But that's disputable, I reckon.

I believe my daddy would of disputed it. He always claimed he was the unluckiest man he knowed of.

That right? Where's he at now? Home I reckon, where you . . .

He's dead.

The squire had propped one foot on the chair before him and was rubbing his paunch abstractedly, watching nothing. His hand stopped and he looked at Holme and looked away again. Well, he said. I guess that's about as unlucky as a feller would be likely to get.

Yessir.

You got ary family a-tall?

I ain't got sign one of kin on this earth, Holme said.

Here, the woman said.

Holme looked vacantly at the steaming plate of eggs before him.

Holler when you get done eatin, the squire said, rising. I'll be out in the back.

All right, Holme said. How long can I stay?

The squire stopped at the door. What? he said.

I said how long can I stay.

The squire shrugged his coat over his shoulders. It's ten days at fifty cents a day. That's all.

What about after that?

What about it.

I mean can I stay on longer?

What for?

Well, just to stay. To work.

At fifty cents a day?

I don't care.

Don't care?

I'll stay on just for board if you can use me.

It was very quiet in the kitchen. The squire was standing with one hand on the door. The woman had stopped her puttering with dishes and pots. They were watching him.

I don't believe I can use ye, Holme, the squire said. Holler when ye get done.

SHE CAME FROM the house onto the porch and stood there taking the soft evening air and smelling the rich ground beyond the road where he followed the mule down the creek and back and down again through a deepening haze, he and the mule alike beset by plovers who pass and wheel and repass and at length give up the long blue dusk to bats. The flowers in the dooryard have curled and drawn as if poisoned by dark and there is a mockingbird to tell what he knows of night.

She sat quietly in the rocker. It was full dark when he came up from the bottoms, stooped under the small Japanese plow, the mule coming behind him in the gloom and the two passing like shades but for the paced hollow clop of the mule's shoeless feet in the road and then the softer sound in the wet grass and the slight chink of harness until they went beyond hearing into the barnlot. She was not even rocking. After a while she heard him in the house and he lit a lamp and came to the porch door and called her. She rose and went in, past him wordlessly and her slippers like mice along the dark hallway until he caught up behind her and lit her way into the kitchen where she began to fix his supper.

He sat at the table watching her, his hands cupped uselessly in his lap and his face red in the lamplight. Watching her move from the stove to the safe and back, mute, shuffling, wooden. When she set the greens and cold pork and milk before him he looked at them dumbly for a long time before he took up his fork and he ate listlessly like a man in sorrow.

She started past him toward the door and he took her by the elbow. Hold up a minute, he said.

She stopped and came about slowly, doll-like, one arm poised. She was not looking at him.

Look here at me. Rinthy.

She swung her eyes vaguely toward him.

You ain't even civil, he said. It ain't civil to come and go thataway and not say nothin never.

I ain't got nothin to say.

Well damn it you could say somethin. Hello or goodbye or kiss my ass. Somethin. Couldn't ye?

I've not took up cussin yet, she said.

Just hello or goodbye then. Couldn't ye?

I reckon.

Well?

Goodnight, she said.

He watched her go, his jaw let down to speak again but not speaking, watched her fade from the reach of the powdery lamplight and heard her steps soft on the moaning stairboards and the wooden clap of the door closing. Goodnight, he said. He drank the last of the milk from the glass and wiped his mouth on his shoulder in a curious birdlike gesture. He'd see all night again tonight the mule's hasped hoofs wristing up before him and the cool earth passing and passing, canting dark and moldy with humus across the coulter with that dull and watery sound interspersed with the click of bedded creekstones.

A moth had got in and floundered at the lamp chimney with great eyed wings, lay prostrate and quivering on the greasy oilcloth tablecover. He crushed it with his fist and flicked it from sight and sat before the empty plate drumming his fingers in the mothshaped swatch of glinting dust it left.

She did not know that she was leaving. She woke in the night and rose half tranced from the bed and began to dress, all in darkness and with gravity. Perhaps some dream had moved her so. She took her few things from the chifforobe and bundled them and went to the landing beyond her door. She listened for his breathing in the room opposite but she could hear nothing. She crouched in the dark long and long for fear he was awake and when she did descend the stairs in her bare feet she paused again at the bottom in the dead black foyer and listened up the stairwell. And she waited again at the front door with it open, poised between the maw of the dead and loveless house and the outer dark like a frail thief. It was damp and cool and she could hear roosters beginning. She closed the door and went down the path to the gate and into the road, shivering in the cold starlight, under vega and the waterserpent.

She went west on the road while the sky grew pale and

the waking world of shapes accrued about her. Hurrying along with the sunrise at her back she had the look of some deranged refugee from its occurrence. Before she had gone far she heard a horse on the road behind her and she fled into the wood with her heart at her throat. It came out of the sun at a slow canter, in a silhouette agonized to shapelessness. She crouched in the bushes and watched it, a huge horse emerging seared and whole from the sun's eye and passing like a wrecked caravel gaunt-ribbed and black and mad with tattered saddle and dangling stirrups and hoofs clopping softly in the dust and passing enormous and emaciate and inflamed and the sound of it dying down the road to a distant echo of applause in a hall forever empty.

On a good spring day he paused to rest at the side of the road. He had been walking for a long time and he had been hearing them for a long time before he knew what the sound was, a faint murmurous droning portending multitudes, locusts, the advent of primitive armies. He rose and went on until he reached the gap in the ridge and before long he could see the first of them coming along the road below him and then suddenly the entire valley was filled with hogs, a weltering sea of them that came smoking over the dusty plain and flowed undiminished into the narrows of the cut, fanning on the slopes in ragged shoals like the harried outer guard of schooled fish and here and there upright and cursing among them and laboring with poles the drovers, gaunt and fever-eyed with incredible rag costumes and wild hair.

Holme left the road and clambered up the rocky slope to give them leeway. The first of the drovers was beating his way obliquely across the herd toward him, the hogs flaring and squealing and closing behind him again like syrup. When he gained the open ground he came along easily, smiling up to where Holme sat on a rock with his feet dangling and looking down with no little wonder at this spectacle.

Howdy neighbor, called out the drover. Sweet day, ain't she?

It is, he said. Whereabouts are ye headed with them hogs if you don't care for me astin?

Crost the mountain to Charlestown.

Holme shook his head reverently. That there is the damndest sight of hogs ever I seen, he said. How many ye got?

The drover had come about the base of the rock and was now standing looking down with Holme at the passing hogs. God hisself don't know, he said solemnly.

Well it's a bunch.

They Lord, said the drover, they just now commencin to come in sight. He passed his stave from the crook of one arm to the other and cocked one foot on the ledge of rock, his sparse whiskers fluttering in the mountain wind, leaning forward and watching the howling polychrome tide of hogs that glutted the valley from wall to wall as might any chance traveler a thing of interest.

They's more than one mulefoot in that lot, he said.

What?

Mulefoot. I calculate they's several hunnerd head of them alone and they ain't no common hog to come upon.

What's a mulefoot? Holme said.

The drover squinted professionally. Mountain hog from north of here. You ain't never seen one?

No.

Got a foot like a mule.

You mean they ain't got a split hoof?

Nary split to it.

I ain't never seen no such hog as that, Holme said.

I ain't surprised, the drover said. But ye can see one here if you've a mind to.

I'd admire to, Holme said.

The drover shifted his stave again. Seems like that don't agree with the bible, what would you say?

About what?

About them hogs. Bein unclean on account of they got a split foot.

I ain't never heard that, Holme said.

I heard it preached in a sermon one time. Feller knowed right smart about the subject. Said the devil had a foot like a hog's. He laid claim it was in the bible so I reckon it's so.

I reckon.

He said a jew wouldn't eat hogmeat on account of it.

What's a jew?

That's one of them old-timey people from in the bible. But that still don't say nothin about a mulefoot hog does it? What about him?

I don't know, Holme said. What about him?

Well is he a hog or ain't he? Accordin to the bible.

I'd say a hog was a hog if he didn't have nary feet a-tall.

I might do it myself, the drover said, because if he was to have feet you'd look for em to be hog's feet. Like if ye had a hog didn't have no head you'd know it for a hog anyways. But if ye seen one walkin around with a mule's head on him ye might be puzzled.

That's true, Holme allowed.

Yessir. Makes ye wonder some about the bible and about hogs too, don't it?

Yes, Holme said.

I've studied it a good deal and I cain't come to no conclusions about it one way or the other.

No.

The drover stroked his whiskers and nodded his head. Hogs is a mystery by theyselves, he said. What can a feller know about one? Not a whole lot. I've run with hogs since I was just a shirttail and I ain't never come to no real understandin of em. And I don't doubt but what other folks has had the same experience. A hog is a hog. Pure and simple. And that's about all ye can say about him. And smart, don't think they ain't. Smart as the devil. And don't be fooled by one that ain't got nary clove foot cause he's devilish too.

I guess hogs is hogs, Holme said.

The drover spat and nodded. That's what I've always maintained, he said.

Holme was watching the activity below them.

That's my little brother Billy yander, the drover said, pointing with one tatterclad arm. This is his first time along. I thought mamma was goin to bawl sure enough when we lit out and him with us. Says he goin to get him some poontang when we get sold but I told him he'd be long done partialed to shehogs. The drover turned and bared his orangecolored teeth at Holme in a grimace of lecherous idiocy. Holme turned and watched the hogs. The drovers stood among them like crossers in a ford, emerging periodically out of the shifting pall of red dust and then blotted away again. They seemed together with the hogs to be in flight from some act of God, fire or flood, schisms in the earth's crust.

I better get on and give them fellers a hand, the drover said.

Luck to ye, Holme said.

We'll be stopped up on the river somewheres come dark. If ye chance by that way just stop and take supper with us.

Thank ye, said Holme. I'd be proud to.

The drover waved his staff and scrabbled away over the rocks like a thin gnome. Holme sat for a while and then rose and followed along the ridge toward the gap where the hogs were crossing.

The gap was narrow and when he got to it he could see the hogs welled up in a clamorous and screeching flume that fanned again on the far side in a high meadow skirting the bluff of the river. They were wheeling faster and wider out along the sheer rim of the bluff in an arc of dusty uproar and he could hear the drovers below him calling and he could see the dead gray serpentine of the river below that. Hogs were pouring through the gap and building against the ones in the meadow until these began to buckle at the edges. Holme saw two of them pitch screaming in stifflegged pirouettes a hundred feet into the river. He moved down the slope toward the bluff and the road that went along it. Drovers were racing brokenly across the milling hogs with staves aloft, stumbling and falling among them, making for the outer perimeter to head them from the cliff. This swept a new wave of panic among the hogs like wind through grass until a whole echelon of them careering up the outer flank forsook the land and faired into space with torn cries. Now the entire herd had begun to wheel wider and faster along the bluff and the outermost ranks swung centrifugally over the escarpment row on row wailing and squealing and above this the howls and curses of the drovers that now upreared in the moil of flesh they tended and swept with dust had begun to assume satanic looks with their staves and wild eyes as if they were no true swineherds but disciples of darkness got among these charges to herd them to their doom.

Holme rushed to higher ground like one threatened with flood and perched upon a rock there to view the course of things. The hogs were in full stampede. One of the drovers passed curiously erect as though braced with a stick and rotating slowly with his arms outstretched in the manner of a dancing sleeper. Hogs were beginning to wash up on the rock, their hoofs clicking and rasping and with harsh snorts. Holme recoiled to the rock's crown and watched them. The drover who had spoken him swept past with bowed back and hands aloft, a limp and ragged scarecrow flailing briefly in that rabid frieze so that Holme saw tilted upon him for just a moment out of the dust and pandemonium two walled eyes beyond hope and a dead mouth beyond prayer, borne on like some old gospel recreant seized sevenfold in the flood of his own nether invocations or grotesque hero bobbing harried and unwilling on the shoulders of a mob stricken in their iniquity to the very shape of evil until he passed over the rim of the bluff and dropped in his great retinue of hogs from sight.

Holme blinked and shook his head. The hogs boiled past squealing and plunging and the chalky red smoke of their passage hung over the river and stained the sky with something of sunset. They had begun to veer from the bluff and to swing in a long arc upriver. The drovers all had sought shelter among the trees and Holme could see a pair of them watching the herd pass with looks of indolent speculation, leaning upon their staves and nodding in mute agreement as if there were some old injustice being righted in this spectacle of headlong bedlam.

When the last of the hogs had gone in a rapidly trebling thunder and the ochreous dust had drifted from the torn ground and there was nothing but quaking silence about him Holme climbed gingerly from his rock. Some drovers were coming from the trees and three pink shoats labored up over the rim of the hill with whimpering sounds not unlike kittens and bobbed past and upriver over the gently smoking land like creatures in a dream.

Holme walked slowly up the bluff. The sun was bright and it was a fine spring day. The drovers had begun to assemble and they seemed in no hurry to overtake the hogs. They were handing about plugs and pouches of tobacco with an indifferent conviviality.

That beats everthing I ever seen, one said.

That's pitiful about your brother.

I don't know what all I'm goin to tell mamma. Herded off

a bluff with a parcel of hogs. I don't know how I'm goin to tell her that.

You could tell her he was drunk.

Tell her he got shot or somethin.

You wouldn't need to tell her he went to his reward with a herd of hogs.

He shook his head sorrowfully. Lord I just don't know, he said. I just wisht I knowed what to tell her.

You won't see her for a couple of months anyways, Billy. Give ye time to think some about it.

What happent? Holme said.

One of the drovers looked at him. They Lord, he said, where was you at? Did you not see them hogs?

I seen him a-settin on a rock over yander, Billy said. Vernon went right past him and he never reached to help him nor nothin.

The drovers looked at him, a bizarre collection of faces that seemed assembled from scraps and oddments, all hairyfaced and filthy and half toothless and their weathered chops lumpy with tobacco chews. One spat and squinted up at Holme.

That right, stranger? he said.

Holme ignored him. I didn't see you comin to help, he said.

I wasn't near him, Billy said. I couldn't of got to him. You was right there.

I seen him a-settin on that rock.

That's all right about him settin on some rock, who was it got them hogs started in the first place?

That's right. How come em to do thataway?

Where was you at, stranger? When them hogs commenced runnin crazy.

I wasn't nowheres. I was way back yander.

Behind em kindly?

He just watched Vernon go right on out over the bluff and never said diddly shit.

Somethin had to of spooked them hogs thataway.

Well ain't he just said he come up behind em?

He never raised hand one to save him.

Stranger we don't take too kind to people runnin off folks' stock.

We ain't got a whole lot of use for troublemakers hereabouts.

Vernon never bothered nobody. You can ast anybody.

Shit, Holme said. You sons of bitches are crazy.

Peace be on all you fellers, a voice sang out behind them. Two of the drovers removed their hats. Holme looked around to see what was occurring.

A parson or what looked like one was laboring over the crest of the hill and coming toward them with one hand raised in blessing, greeting, fending flies. He was dressed in a dusty frockcoat and carried a walking stick and he wore a pair of octagonal glasses on the one pane of which the late sun shone while a watery eye peered from the naked wire aperture of the other.

What's the ruckus here? Hey? He drew up and looked from one to the other among them and looked at the ground as if he had forgotten something, taking a kerchief from his sleeve and snorting into it.

Howdy Reverend, said Billy.

Howdy. Bless all of ye'ns. They Lord what's been thew here?

Hogs, said one of the drovers. Damndest mess of hogs you ever seen, excuse me.

Hard words don't bother me no more than does hard ways, said the reverend. That's what all I'm here for. What's he done? You ain't fixin to hang him are ye? Vengeance is mine sayeth the Lord. Don't hold with hangin a-tall lessen it's legal. What possessed them hogs anyways?

This here feller run em off, Billy said.

I never done it, Holme said.

The hell you never.

Here now, somebody's lyin. You, young feller, look me in the eye and tell me you never run them hogs off.

I never run em off, Holme said.

The drovers pressed about to watch.

The preacher looked at the ground again, stuffing the kerchief back up his sleeve.

Well, Reverend?

I believe he run em off.

I told ye, Billy said.

Goddamn it, Holme said, I wasn't nowheres . . .

Watch that talk in front of the preacher, boy, one of the drovers said.

But don't hang him boys, the reverend said. Don't do it.

We'll take him in to justice. Render unto Caesar what all's hisn.

He shoved brother Billy's brother Vernon off the bluff with the hogs.

Just a goddamn minute, Holme said.

There he goes again with that mouth.

Don't hang him, boys, the preacher cried out. No good'll ever come of it.

Everbody seen what he done, Billy said. You all seen it.

The preacher looked like a charred bird. He was peering at the ground and pounding his cane there. Ah don't hang him, he said. Oh Lord don't hang him. Shaking his head and muttering these things loudly over and over.

It's a serious thing, the preacher said. I don't advocate it save under the strongest extremes.

Well if you'd hush about it . . .

Tore up with guilt. The preacher nodded sad and negative. Plumb tore up with it.

We all seen him on that rock.

How come ye to do it, son?

Holme looked about him for some sign of sanity. Shit, he said.

I believe we done mentioned it to ye oncet about that barnyard talk.

The preacher had begun to gesture inanely with his cane. Boys I believe he's plumb eat up with the devil in him. But don't hang him.

Ort to thow him off the bluff the way he done Vernon, Billy said.

How far down is it? the preacher was interested.

Too far to walk back.

Billy don't know what all to tell his maw, Reverend. He just don't have no notion how to go about tellin her. Ain't that right Billy?

I don't know what none of us is goin to tell Greene come upon his hogs. They must of been two hunnerd head fell off in the river.

Don't flang him off the bluff, boys, the preacher said. I believe ye'd be better to hang him as that.

I believe we would too.

What do you say Billy? He's your brother.

I believe I'd rest easier. I believe Vernon would of wanted it thataway.

Lessen he's got some choice.

They looked at Holme.

Vernon never had none, Billy said.

He's right about that.

Well he probably don't care noway. You got any particulars, stranger? Strung up or flang off in the river?

Holme wiped his palms down the sides of his overall legs and looked about him with wide eyes.

Let's hang him if he don't care. I ain't never seen nobody hung.

We ain't got nary rope.

They stopped and looked from one to the other.

Rope?

Cain't hang him thout a rope.

They's one in the wagon. Cecil's got one in the wagon.

They Lord he'll be ten mile up the river fore we catch him.

He'll be stopped makin camp now late as it is. We hurry we can get up there and get him hung afore dark.

Let's just thow him off the bluff and be done with it.

Naw, that ain't no way to do. Besides Billy wants him hung.

I believe Vernon would of wanted it thataway, Billy said.

I believe old Greene'll be comforted some too.

Don't flang him off the bluff, boys. Tain't christian.

Let's go then.

Hump up there, stranger, and let's go get hung.

They started up the river.

The preacher fell in alongside Holme. What place of devilment you hail from, mister? he asked.

Holme looked at him wearily. I don't come from no place of devilment, he said. I come from Johnson County.

Never heard tell of it. You a christian?

Yes.

I cain't say as you've much took on the look of one.

It ain't marked you a whole lot to notice neither, Holme said.

Don't disperge the cloth son, the preacher said. Don't disperge the cloth.

Cloth's ass, Holme said.

Well now, said the preacher, what have we here. I believe it's a hard enough case to give Jehovah hisself the witherins.

Holme didn't answer.

Might be somethin of a comfort to have a preacher there

at your final hour, the preacher went on. If your heart ain't just scabbed over with sin.

You don't look like much of a preacher to me, Holme said.

I'll bet I don't, the preacher said. I'd just bet I don't at that, to you.

Holme trudged along over the chopped ground. They were following the swath the hogs had made.

Where was it you was a-goin anyways? the preacher asked.

Just on to the next town.

Guess you never reckoned when ye set out this mornin that you was on your way to be hung. Did ye?

Holme ignored him.

A feller never knows what day'll be his last in this vale of tears. You been baptized?

Why don't you go on and walk somewheres else? Holme said.

I guess a feller mires up so deep in sin after a while he don't want to hear nothin about grace and salvation. Not even a feller about to be hung dead.

It ain't no use, Reverend. He's too mean to be saved.

Most probably you right, the reverend said. But I sure would love to do it if I could. It'd make a jimdandy sermon. I saved a blind feller once wanted to curse God for his affliction. You all want to hear that'n? It's a strong sermon. I like to save it for best.

Tell it, Reverend.

I won't tell it all. This blind feller hollered out one time and said: Looky here at me, blind and all. I guess you reckon I ort to love Jesus.

Well neighbor, I says, I believe ye ort. He give ye eyes to see and then he tuck em away. And maybe you never was much of a christian to start with and he figgered this'd bring ye round. They's been more than one feller brought to the love of Jesus over the paths of affliction. And what better way than blind? In a world darksome as this'n I believe a blind man ort to be better sighted than most. I believe it's got a good deal to recommend it. The grace of God don't rest easy on a man. It can blind him easy as not. It can bend him and make him crooked. And who did Jesus love, friends? The lame the halt and the blind, that's who; Them is the ones scarred with God's mercy. Stricken with his love. Ever legless fool and old blind mess like you is a flower in the garden of God. Amen. I told him that.

That's a right pretty sermon, Reverend.

I wisht Vernon could of heard it.

He knelt right there and was saved on the spot, the reverend said.

The path had come down from the high bluffs and was going along the river and already it was late afternoon. Holme looked about, stepped past the preacher and the drover next him and jumped.

It was a long way down and when he hit he felt something tear in his leg. He came up with a mouthful of muddy water and spat and turned. They were aligned along the bluff watching him. The preacher had both hands aloft, gesturing. The drovers against the pale sky were small, erect, simian shapes. The seven of them watched him. He could hear the preacher's voice. The current was carrying him on and his leg was hurting but he kept watching them and after a while they were very small and then they turned and went on along the bluff with no order rank or valence to anything in the shapen world.

WHAT DISCORDANT vespers do the tinker's goods chime through the long twilight and over the brindled forest road, him stooped and hounded through the windy recrements of day like those old exiles who divorced of corporeality and enjoined ingress of heaven or hell wander forever the middle warrens spoorless increate and anathema. Hounded by grief, by guilt, or like this cheerless vendor clamored at heel through wood and fen by his own querulous and inconsolable wares in perennial tin malediction.

In the clearing he set down his cart and circled the remains of a fire out of which rose a slender stem of smoke like the pistil of a burnt flower, his thin nose constricted and eyes wary. Shapes of risen sleepers lay in the pressed and poisoned grass. He set out the child and gathered wood and built back the fire. Dark fell and bats came to hunt the glade, crossing above the figure sulking there on his gaunt shanks like little voiceless souls. Then they went away. A fox stopped barking. The tinker in his mothgnawn blanket nodded. The child slept.

The three men when they came might have risen from the ground. The tinker could not account for them. They gathered about the fire and looked down at him. One had a rifle and was smiling. Howdy, the tinker said.

HOLME CAME LIMPING out of the woods and crossed a small field toward the light, insects rising out of the dark and breaking on his face like rain and his fingers trailing in the tops of the wet sedge. He could hear no sound save a faint moaning like the wind but there was no wind. When he entered the glade he could see men seated about the fire and he hobbled on, one hand raised, into the firelight. When he saw what figures warmed there he was already among them and it was too late. There were three of them and there was a child squatting in the dust and beyond them the tinker's cart with the hung pans catching the light like the baleful eyes of some outsized and mute and mindless jury assembled there hurriedly against his coming.

Howdy, said the bearded one. Ain't seen ye for a while.

He looked at them. They wore the same clothes, sat in the same attitudes, endowed with a dream's redundancy. Like revenants that reoccur in lands laid waste with fever: spectral, palpable as stone. He looked at the child. It had a healed burn all down one side of it and the skin was papery and wrinkled like an old man's. It was naked and half coated with dust so that it seemed lightly furred and when it turned to look up at him he saw one eyeless and angry red socket like a stokehole to a brain in flames. He looked away.

Set and rest a spell, the man said.

Holme squatted, favoring his off leg. The child kept watching him.

Whose youngern? he said.

Harmon guffawed and slapped his thigh.

What happent to his eye? Holme said.

What eye.

His eye. He gestured. The one he ain't got.

I reckon he must of lost it somewheres. He still got one.

He ort to have two.

Maybe he ort to have more'n that. Some folks has two and cain't see.

Holme didn't say anything.

I reckon that tinker might know what happent to it.

What tinker?

That'n in yan tree, said Harmon, pointing with the rifle.

Hush. Don't pay him no mind mister. What did ye do to your leg there?

Nothin.

The bearded one was tunneling gouts of mud from the welt of his boot with a stick. Well, I see ye didn't have no trouble findin us.

I wasn't huntin ye.

You got here all right for somebody bound elsewhere.

I wasn't bound nowheres. I just seen the fire.

I like to keep a good fire. A man never knows what all might chance along. Does he?

No.

No. Anything's liable to warsh up. From nowheres nowhere bound.

Where are you bound? Holme said.

I ain't, the man said. By nothin. He looked up at Holme. We ain't hard to find. Oncet you've found us.

Holme looked away. His sweatblistered forehead shone in the firelight. He looked toward the tinker's cart and he looked at the child. Where's she at? he said.

Who's that?

My sister.

Ah, said the man. The one run off with that tinker.

Them's his traps yander.

The bearded one turned his head slightly and looked and turned back. Aye, he said. That'n you used to trade with.

I never give him no chap, Holme said. I just told her that.

Maybe thisn's some other chap.

It ain't nothin to me.

The bearded one raked a gobbet of clay from his stick and cast it into the fire. You know what I figure? he said.

What.

I figure you got this thing here in her belly your own self and then laid it off on that tinker.

I never laid nothin off on no tinker.

I reckon you figured he'd keep him hid for ye.

I never figured nothin.

What did ye have to give him?

I never give nobody nothin. I never had nothin.

Never figured nothin, never had nothin, never was nothin, the man said. He was looking at nothing at all. The mute one seemed to sleep, crouched at the man's right with his arms dangling between his knees like something waiting to be wakened and fed.

What are you? Holme muttered.

What?

He said it again, sullenly.

The bearded one smiled. Ah, he said. Now. We've heard that before, ain't we?

You ain't nothin to me.

But the man didn't seem to hear. He nodded as if spoken by other voices. He didn't look at Holme.

You never did say what you done with your sister.

I never done nothin with her.

Where's she at?

I don't know. She run off.

You done told that.

It ain't nothin to you.

I'll be the judge of that.

Harmon turned, his cheek against the upright rifle-barrel. He smiled dreamily.

I reckon little sister's just a little further on up the road, ain't she? the man said.

I don't know. I ain't seen her.

No.

I allowed maybe you had, Holme said. You seem to know everbody's business.

I guess it ain't nothin to me. Is that right?

Holme didn't answer.

The man wiped the stick and poked it into the fire and stretched forth his boot. Hand him here, he said.

What?

Hand him here. Yan chap.

Holme didn't move. The child had not stopped watching him.

Unless you'd rather for Harmon to.

He looked at Harmon and then he bent forward and picked up the child. It made no gesture at all. It dangled from his hands like a dressed rabbit, a gross eldritch doll with ricketsprung legs and one eye opening and closing softly like a naked owl's. He rose with it and circled the fire and held it out toward the man. The man looked at it a moment and then took it with one hand by its upper arm and placed it between his feet.

What do you want with him? Holme said.

Nothin. No more than you do.

He ain't nothin to me.

No.

Where's that tinker at if he was raisin him?

He's all raised out. He cain't raise no more.

You don't need him.

Water in the summer and fire in the winter is all the need I need. We ain't talkin about what I need. He spat across the child's head into the fire and a thin chain of sparks ascended in the graygreen smoke. That ain't what's concerned.

No.

You ain't no different from the rest. From any man borned and raised and have his own and die. They ain't one man in three got even a black suit to die in.

Holme stood with his feet together and his hands at his sides like one arraigned.

What's his name? the man said.

I don't know.

He ain't got nary'n.

No. I don't reckon. I don't know.

They say people in hell ain't got names. But they had to be called somethin to get sent there. Didn't they.

That tinker might of named him.

It wasn't his to name. Besides names dies with the namers. A dead man's dog ain't got a name. He reached and drew from his boot a slender knife.

Holme seemed to be speaking to something in the night beyond them all. My sister would take him, he said. That chap. We could find her and she'd take him.

Yes, the man said.

I been huntin her.

Harmon was watching the man. Even the mute one stirred. The man took hold of the child and lifted it up. It was watching the fire. Holme saw the blade wink in the light like a long cat's eye slant and malevolent and a dark smile erupted on the child's throat and went all broken down the front of it. The child made no sound. It hung there with its one eye glazing over like a wet stone and the black blood pumping down its naked belly. The mute one knelt forward. He was drooling and making little whimpering noises in his throat.

He knelt with his hands outstretched and his nostrils rimpled delicately. The man handed him the child and he seized it up, looked once at Holme with witless eyes, and buried his moaning face in its throat.

Late in the afternoon she entered the glade, coming down a footpath where narrow cart tracks had crushed the weeds and through the wood, half wild and haggard in her shapeless sundrained cerements, yet delicate as any fallow doe, and so into the clearing to stand cradled in a grail of jade and windy light, slender and trembling and pale with wandlike hands to speak the boneless shapes attending her.

And stepping softly with her air of blooded ruin about the glade in a frail agony of grace she trailed her rags through dust and ashes, circling the dead fire, the charred billets and chalk bones, the little calcined ribcage. She poked among the burnt remains of the tinker's traps, the blackened pans confused among the rubble, the lantern with its skewed glass, the axle and iron wheelhoops already rusting. She went among this charnel curiously. She did not know what to make of it. She waited, but no one returned.

She waited all through the blue twilight and into the dark. Bats came and went. Wind stirred the ashes and the tinker in his tree turned slowly but no one returned. Shadows grew cold across the wood and night rang down upon these lonely figures and after a while little sister was sleeping.

The tinker in his burial tree was a wonder to the birds. The vultures that came by day to nose with their hooked beaks among his buttons and pockets like outrageous pets soon left him naked of his rags and flesh alike. Black mandrake sprang beneath the tree as it will where the seed of the hanged falls and in spring a new branch pierced his breast and flowered in a green boutonniere perennial beneath his yellow grin. He took the sparse winter snows upon what thatch of hair still clung to his dried skull and hunters that passed that way never chanced to see him brooding among his barren limbs. Until wind had tolled the tinker's bones and seasons loosed them one by one to the ground below and alone his bleached and weathered brisket hung in that lonesome wood like a bone birdcage.

IN LATER YEARS he used to meet a blind man, ragged and serene, who spoke him a good day out of his constant dark. He overtook him tapping through the bright noon dust with his cane, his head erect in that air of wonder the blind wear. Holme would go by but now the blind man has stopped him with his greeting.

How you, said Holme.

Well as ever, said the blind man. Have ye a smoke?

No sir. I ain't.

Nary a-tall?

I don't have the habit.

Aye, said the blind man. He unbuttoned the bib of his overalls and brought forth tobacco. Well, he said, it's good to see the sun again ain't it.

Holme looked at the cups of blue phlegm which regarded him. It is, he said.

Aye. After so long a time. He trickled tobacco into the slender trough of paper his fingers held and put away the pouch.

It is a right pretty day, Holme said.

The blind man smiled. I know ye, he said. I've spoke afore with ye.

You might of, Holme said. I don't remember.

The blind man twisted up the ends of his cigarette and took it between his lips. Yes, he said. I've passed ye on these roads afore.

They's lots of people on the roads these days, Holme said.

Yes, the blind man said. I pass em ever day. People goin up and down in the world like dogs. As if they wasn't a home nowheres. But I knowed I'd seen ye afore.

Holme spat. I got to get on, he said.

Yes, the blind man said. Is they anything you need?

Need?

Anything you need.

I don't need nothin.

I always like to ast.

What are ye sellin?

I ain't sellin nothin. I'm at the Lord's work. He don't need your money.

It's good he don't need mine. I reckon you're some kind of a preacher.

No. No preacher. What is they to preach? It's all plain enough. Word and flesh. I don't hold much with preachin.

Holme smiled. What have you got to give? Old blind man like you astin folks what they need.

I don't know. Nobody's never said.

Well how would you expect to get it.

Just pray for it.

You always get what you pray for?

Yes. I reckon. I wouldn't pray for what wasn't needful. Would you?

I ain't never prayed. Why don't ye pray back your eyes?

I believe it'd be a sin. Them old eyes can only show ye what's done there anyways. If a blind man needed eyes he'd have eyes.

Still I believe you'd like to see your way.

What needs a man to see his way when he's sent there anyhow?

I got to get on, Holme said.

The blind man leaned one hand on the cane where he had rested it against his leg. He sucked on the cigarette and two jets of blue smoke slid from his thin nostrils and faded in the air. I heard a preacher in a town one time, he said. A healin preacher wanted to cure everbody and they took me up there. They was a bunch of us there all cripple folks and one old man they did claim had thowed down his crutches and they told it he could make the blind see. And they was a feller leapt up and hollered out that nobody knowed what was wrong with. And they said it caused that preacher to go away. But they's darksome ways afoot in this world and it may be he weren't no true preacher.

I got to get on, Holme said.

I always did want to find that feller, the blind man said. And tell him. If somebody don't tell him he never will have no rest.

I'll see ye, Holme said.

Aye, said the blind man. It might be we'll meet again sometime.

Holme raised a hand in inane farewell and set off down the road again. The blind man's cane softly tapping faded behind him. He went on, soundless with his naked feet, shambling, gracelorn, down out of the peaceful mazy fields, his toed tracks soft in the dust among the cratered shapes of horse and mule hoofs and before him under the high afternoon sun his shadow be-wandered in a dark parody of his progress. The road went on through a shadeless burn and for miles there were only the charred shapes of trees in a dead land where nothing moved save windy rifts of ash that rose dolorous and died again down the blackened corridors.

Late in the day the road brought him into a swamp. And that was all. Before him stretched a spectral waste out of which reared only the naked trees in attitudes of agony and dimly hominoid like figures in a landscape of the damned. A faintly smoking garden of the dead that tended away to the earth's curve. He tried his foot in the mire before him and it rose in a vulvate welt claggy and sucking. He stepped back. A stale wind blew from this desolation and the marsh reeds and black ferns among which he stood clashed softly like things chained. He wondered why a road should come to such a place.

Going back the way by which he came he met again the blind man tapping through the dusk. He waited very still by the side of the road, but the blind man passing turned his head and smiled upon him his blind smile. Holme watched him out of sight. He wondered where the blind man was going and did he know how the road ended. Someone should tell a blind man before setting him out that way.